Mother

Hristina Bloomfield

Mother

London, 2024

hrisisart@gmail.com

Instagram: @hristinabloomfield

www.authorhristinabloomfield.com

'Rado, you won't sell her, will you? Please! Please!' Thea cried, as she stretched out her hands to her child.

'Go inside and don't cause problems,' her brother said rudely and pushed her on the old armchair. Thea cried out in pain but quickly recovered and tried to go out into the street again to find Maria. When she went outside, she saw that her mother and the baby were no longer there. Thea looked around, but they were nowhere to be seen. Then she heard a baby cry again, coming from the house next door. Their neighbours would help with the 'deal'; she was horrified. Thea had heard of two such deals so far, but in those cases, the mothers were willingly selling their children, for a 'better life'. But she desperately wanted her child and was willing to watch and care for her.

'Why are you doing this to me?' Thea cried and ignoring all the pain she tried to get out of the living room window. However, Rado saw her again, entered the house and this time even more roughly, grabbing her by the hair, pulled her into the bedroom and pushed her onto the bed.

'Why didn't you sell your child but chose to sell mine?' Thea asked him angrily.

'My child is not a bastard; it is mine and has a father.'

'And my child has a father.'

'Yes, she has a great father. Do you know where her father is now? Ha, of course, you don't know. He went to fetch your baby's future parents.'

'You're lying! You're lying!'

'I'm not lying! They will arrive soon, and you will see for yourself.'

'You're lying!' Thea cried, but she knew in her heart that Rado was telling the truth. She had realized too late what kind of person Georgi was. She wasn't the first he'd played like that.

'The family that will take her is very rich. She will be well taken care of, Thea.'

'I will take good care of her. Please don't sell her. Please!'

'You can't take care of her alone. This child will be another mouth we will have to feed.'

'You won't have to feed us; I'll go and take care of her.'

'And where will you go?' Rado asked.

'I will go to Bolengrad. My teacher Mrs. Mariola promised to shelter me if necessary.'

'You won't go anywhere. So far, we have endured you. Do you know how much money you're costing us? No, you will never be able to pay us back.'

'At least let me hug her,' Thea begged.

'No, her new parents specifically mentioned that you were not to breastfeed or hold her. According to them, this will cause you to back out of the deal.'

'Please, Rado! Please! Let me see her for a little while.'

'No!' he shouted and left the room.

Thea stood up again and rested her head against the window. They had all returned and sat again on the old bench in the street. The baby continued to cry, and Thea's mother tried to calm it down. Then her neighbour took her, but she couldn't stop the baby's crying either. The men next to them got nervous and started shouting. Only fragmentary words reached Thea. According to the neighbour, they had to feed the baby to calm her down. Thea watched her daughter, whose face was red from crying, and her heart ached. She gathered her strength again and started towards the living room. She was just reaching for the doorknob when her mother came in with the baby. Thea held out her arms to her daughter, and to her surprise, her mother let her take her.

'You have to feed her to stop crying.'

Thea hugged her daughter. Then she sat down on the old armchair and instinctively began to nurse Maria.

'Don't get attached; she won't stay with us. Georgi is coming soon with her new parents.'

Thea's eyes watered. She watched her baby feed and stroked her. At the curve of Maria's neck near her left shoulder, Thea noticed a birthmark. She tried to remember it without looking for long, so that her mother would not notice her memorising her baby's skin.

After feeding, the baby calmed down and drifted off to sleep. Her small lips parted slightly, and to Thea, it was the most beautiful thing she had ever seen. She stared like that, trying not to think about what might happen soon. She just stared at her daughter, enjoying the moment.

The sound of an oncoming car startled Thea's mother. She got up quickly, took the baby from Thea's arms, and tried to go outside. Thea held her back and tried to take the baby back, but her brother appeared and pushed her inside the house.

'No! No!' Thea shouted. Rado approached her and ordered her to shut up through his teeth. However, she did not give up. She shouted as loud as she could so that the people who wanted to buy her baby could hear her. She rapped on the window to get their attention, and Thea saw an elderly couple get out of the car and turn to the shouting in the house. But then they continued, ignoring her, and the woman took the baby in her arms. Georgi was standing on the side and smiling. Not even looking at his child. All the time he was watching the 'buyers' and talking about something with them. Thea started screaming again. This time she tried to break the window. The slap Rado gave her stopped her. Her brother pushed her to the ground and leaned into one of her ears.

'If you don't stop screaming, I'll kill you,' he said through gritted teeth. Then he roughly lifted her off the ground and pushed her onto the bed.

Thea tried to get out and see what was going on through the window, but every time she got out of bed, Rado pushed her back roughly, and finally she felt so tired that she didn't have the strength to stand up.

Shortly after, she heard the car start, and her heart felt as though it might shatter. She could feel the absence of her daughter without even having to see with her own eyes that she was no longer there. They had sold her, and the old couple had taken her. Thea stared at the cracked ceiling wall. Tears were falling from her eyes, but she couldn't feel them. What she felt right now was helplessness. She closed her eyes and wished herself dead. She couldn't live without her daughter. Then Thea remembered the little body clinging to her as she nursed and told herself she wanted to feel that again. She would find her; she would fight for her and bring her back into her life. She knew what the people who took her looked like, and she would turn every corner of the world to find them and get her back.

2

After a hard, emotional day, Thea finally fell asleep. She woke up several times from the nightmares she was having. At one point, she heard her family feasting in the living room. Her father and brother had gotten drunk and were swearing at their wives. Thea was ashamed of them, ashamed of her family and ashamed of what they had done. She wanted to make a plan and escape as quickly as possible from this house. But where would she go, she wondered. There should be someone somewhere on this earth who would agree to help her, she thought, and she became so carried away with her plans that she flitted between sleeping and waking all night long.

When she woke for the final time, she was full of doubt and fear. The house was quiet now. Her relatives and neighbours had feasted late and were now asleep. Thea opened the door to the living room, praying the old hinges wouldn't creak. When she looked into the room, she saw only her father. He was lying on the old sofa, snoring loudly. Her mother was nowhere to be seen; she had probably gone shopping with Rado to the twenty-four-hour store in Bolengrad, Thea thought. She went back into the bedroom, put on the old pants she had worn while pregnant, threw on a sweater quickly, and went back into the living room quietly. Her winter jacket was hanging on the hanger under her father's coat. Thea decided not to take any chances and by reaching for her own coat slowly unhooked his, slipped it on, and slowly opened the front door. Then she crossed herself twice before going out and prayed her neighbours wouldn't see her.

Her parents' house was the sixth in the row of houses, and the smallest property in the hamlet. Thea went out the front door and quickly moved to the back of the house, which was full of all kinds of hardware and junk. If anyone had seen her, they would have thought she was out on the road, but that wasn't Thea's intention. She wanted to use the rubbish in the backyard for temporary cover and, if no one was looking for her right away, slip through the broken wooden fence and into the woods that were behind the hamlet.

Thea stood silently for a minute, listening to see if anyone had followed her. She heard no voices or footsteps, so she slipped through the hole in the fence and found herself in a small meadow with two horses owned by one of their neighbours. The horses grazed peacefully as she walked past them and entered the forest. The pain in her groin prevented her from walking quickly, and Thea made slow progress. Several miles separated her hamlet from the town. She knew the way there very well because she had walked that way for over ten years. Every weekday morning, except for the holidays, Thea took her backpack with her textbooks and notebooks and walked to the town school. It took her about an hour to get there. She often arrived at school with muddy shoes, wet and frozen from the cold, but when she got there, she was comforted and calm.

For many years Thea thought of the school as her own home. Her classmates made fun of her looks and called her names, but she was used to their taunts. For a long time, insults from her peers did not affect her. The only opinion that mattered to Thea was that of the teachers, especially Mrs. Mariola. The teacher had taken her under her wing, and now, walking to her house, Thea was thinking how right Mrs. Mariola had been when she had warned her about Georgi.

'He's a bad guy, Thea. You deserve more,' she had told her, but Thea did not listen to her. She was so in love and blinded that she turned her back on the old woman and stopped contacting her.

I'm so stupid, Thea thought, and tears began to flow down her face. She walked off the path and jumped over bushes and stumps. Thea knew that it was likely that her family had already found out that she had escaped and would have started looking for her. The path to town would be the first place they would check, so she decided to take a detour that led to the more distant part of Bolengrad. It was a risky decision because it would take her longer to go there, but she had to take the chance to get out. Her plan was to get to her teacher's house, tell her what happened, and seek shelter, at least for a while.

It got cold in the forest, and snow started falling from the sky. *That's not good*, Thea thought. If it piled up, her brother and father would see her steps. She looked up and prayed that it would stop snowing. But instead, the snowfall intensified and turned into a blizzard. Thea wrapped herself further in her father's winter coat and continued to move slowly. She could feel the cold coming from her toes. The shoes she had on were not suitable for bad weather, but she tried to ignore the cold. Instead, she focused on the memory of nursing her daughter. The little gentle body snuggled up to her. That memory warmed Thea, and she kept walking. After about half an hour, she found herself at the edge of the town. Smoke was billowing from the chimneys of the houses. The streets were deserted; no one wanted to go out on a day like this, and since it was Sunday, most people were resting. Everyone preferred to stay warm at home. She hoped her daughter was somewhere warm right now too, Thea thought, looking around cautiously before crossing to the other sidewalk.

Mrs. Mariola's house was located in the central part of the town near the school where Thea had studied until recently. To get there, she had to cross almost half the city. There was no direct way; she could go through several side streets, but in the end, she had to cross the main one. Thea huddled against one of the houses, feeling the warmth of the building's outer wall. She rested her fingers on it, trying to warm them. Then, seeing that someone was approaching her, she quickly lowered her head and went to the other side of the street. The blizzard continued and made the people she passed walk with their heads down. No one looked at her.

Two blocks before the teacher's house, she slowed down and tried to see if anyone from the hamlet was watching the house. Her brother knew Thea was close to this woman and would probably come check on her there. There was no one at the first block, but when she arrived at the street where the teacher's house was, she saw the front door open and Georgi talking to her. Thea's heart sank in fear. Her ex-boyfriend must have gone to threaten Mrs. Mariola, she thought, and wondered where else she could go. Thea looked around and saw the school. She could go in there temporarily, she thought, and headed that way. Thea was horrified to see her brother Rado was standing in front of the school entrance, talking to someone on the phone. She flinched at the sight of his angry face and quickly backed away.

'Thea?' She heard a woman's voice behind her. The voice startled her, and she quickly turned to see who it was, preparing to defend herself. In front of her she saw an old woman, one of Mrs. Mariola's neighbours. Thea had seen her at the teacher's house, but she had never spoken to her and did not remember her name. She only knew that they were friends and sometimes had coffee together.

'Don't be afraid, please and don't run. Mariola called me half an hour ago. She said that all the people from the hamlet are looking for you and asked me to shelter you if I saw you.'

The old woman pushed Thea in front of her and gestured for her to move. After a few houses, Thea saw an open front door and the woman pushed her firmly into the house.

'I think no one saw us,' she said. 'I'm Jeanne, we've met at Mariola's, haven't we? Come, sit near the stove to warm yourself.'

Thea had already headed for the stove and held out her freezing hands to warm herself. Then realizing that she had entered the house with her shoes on, she took them off. The old woman looked at her reddened bare feet from the cold, went into the next room, and returned with hand-knitted warm woollen socks.

'Put them on – they will warm your feet quickly.'

Thea put them on and sat in the chair in front of the stove. 'Thank you,' she said quietly and cried. The warmth and cosiness of the house made her relax, and it caused an outburst of feelings.

'Everything will be okay,' said Jeanne and stroked the crying young woman on the head.

'They took her,' Thea said, sobbing.

'Who did they take?'

'My daughter.'

'Surely, they will return her to you, don't you think?'

'They won't give her back to me. They sold her to a childless family.'

The old lady took a deep breath in surprise. She had heard of babies being sold but thought those stories were just rumours.

'I have to find her.' Thea continued to cry. 'I have to find my daughter.'

'Do you know who took her?'

'I saw them. An elderly couple. I will never forget their faces.'

'Then we'll go to the police. They will investigate. In which hospital did you give birth? The maternity ward will confirm that you gave birth to a girl, isn't it?'

'Only the midwife can confirm. I gave birth in my parents' house.'

'Do you have a birth certificate?' asked Jeanne, trying to understand what happened.

'No, I gave birth, and shortly after that, they took her. I named her Maria.'

The old woman looked at the crying mother and thought that what she had gotten herself into was dangerous. These people were going to look for Thea, and if they found her in her house, who knows what they were going to do to her.

'We have to find a way for you to go to the police or somewhere else. You can't stay here,' Jeanne said quietly.

Thea looked at the old woman and saw the fear in her eyes. It was right for her to be afraid. Thea's brother and father were famous in the town. If they found out that Jeanne had helped her, they would probably take her into the house and beat her up. Only now did Thea realize that her actions would have consequences for anyone who helped her. She got up from the chair, about to take off the warm socks, but Jeanne gestured for her not to. Thea put on her old shoes and silently headed for the front door.

'No, leave this way,' said Jeanne and opened the door to the back yard. 'You can go to Mariola's house from here. Exit here and then to the left. I believe she's expecting you and has left the gate unlocked. If it's locked, you'll find the key under the doormat.'

'Thanks!'

'Good luck, Thea. I hope you find your daughter.'

'Sooner or later, I will find her,' said Thea, opening the garden gate.

The moment Thea closed it behind her, she wondered if she should go to her teacher's house. One of her relatives was probably already there waiting for her. Thea looked around and turned right towards the school. There was an alarm in the school itself, and Thea knew there was no way she could get inside without being noticed, but there was a steam room next to the school building. Every weekday morning, except for holidays, a staff member went to turn on the heater early in the morning. By now the room would be empty, and no one would go inside. Thea knew this because she had used it as a hiding place before. The chance of her being found there was slim to none. The blizzard outside had picked up, and Thea thought that it helped somewhat that no one could see her. She walked around the back of the school building and then headed for the steam room, first checking to see if anyone was standing outside the entrance. Seeing no one, Thea crept to the side and opened a small iron door painted as white as the building, almost invisible unless you knew it was there. The door had been used before coal was brought in more quickly, but as the boiler had long ceased to use coal, the staff at the school did not use it and probably did not even know it had been left unlocked.

Thea entered the dark, windowless room and immediately sat down on the floor. She was very tired, and her loins and legs ached. The lack of an escape plan was giving her a severe headache. *What am I going to do now?* she wondered. *Where will I go?* She could not stay long in this steam room. In the morning, someone would still come and find her here. She needed a new plan, but her hunger and cold prevented her from thinking. Thea curled up into a ball and began to cry softly. She wept for her child, lamented her fate, and cursed herself for allowing all this to happen. And it was all his fault. Georgi was the reason. Her hatred for him grew with each passing minute. *How stupid I have been,* she raged, and her anger stopped her tears for a moment. Then they flowed even more, and this time Thea cried, and a voice of despair rose from her. Her small, pain-ridden body shook with her sobs, and she finally fell to the ground.

After half an hour, her crying finally subsided, and Thea calmed down. She leaned against the cold wall and tried to find a way out of the situation. She was just about to get up and start moving to get warm when the door opened, and someone walked in.

'Thea?' She heard Mrs. Mariola's voice. 'I know you're here. I won't turn on the light, so they don't see us.'

Thea didn't answer right away but waited to see if anyone else would follow the teacher. After no one entered, she approached Mrs. Mariola and lightly touched her hand.

'Thank God!' said Mrs. Mariola. 'Jeanne said you left for my house, but after you didn't come, I decided that you came to hide here again.'

'Did you know I was coming here?' Thea was surprised.

'Most teachers know. The window of the teachers' room looks this way.'

Thea nodded. Of course, she knew the window overlooked the steam room, but she had always come here late in the evening and assumed the teachers had already gone home.

'If my family finds out that you are with me, they might harm you.'

'Don't worry about it. I had a relative of mine tell them that he saw you on the road to Sofia, and they are currently looking for you there.'

'Thanks for the help.'

'What happened? Where is your baby?'

'They sold her.'

Mariola first took a breath of surprise, then exhaled slowly and did something she hadn't done in many years – she swore several times. Then she approached Thea and hugged her. 'Who sold her?'

'All of them, but Georgi had made the deal.'

'I warned you about him.'

'I know, you were right. I'm sorry I didn't believe you.'

The two women sat in the dark in silence for a while.

'We have to go to the police,' Mrs. Mariola finally said. 'Do you have any proof of birth?'

'No. My brother took many pictures of Maria and sent them to Georgi.'

'Maria?'

'My daughter. She has a birthmark on her neck.'

'So, you have proof, but it's not on you?'

'Yes. Roza, the midwife, helped me with the birth, but she will not admit it. They probably paid her, and I think it's not the first time she helps in similar situations.'

'We need to go to the police as soon as possible, Thea. Or call them to come here.' Mariola reached to take her mobile phone out of her pocket, but then she remembered that she had left it at home. 'Come, we'll go through the side streets,' she said and went outside. The blizzard had stopped; only a few stray snowflakes flew by.

Thea and Mrs. Mariola headed for the back of the school. The teacher turned and saw that their steps were visible. There was no way they could cover their tracks, and she was sure that soon Thea's family would find out that the two had been here.

'We must move faster,' said Mrs. Mariola and almost ran. The two women walked past the town's fire station and approached the police building when they noticed Georgi watching them from the opposite sidewalk.

'Run,' Mrs. Mariola said and headed towards Georgi, hoping to block his path to the young woman. Thea hesitated for a second, then ran as fast as she could, panting into the police station. A few seconds later, Mrs. Mariola followed her, followed by Georgi.

Thea looked around and was surprised to see that there was no one in the room she found herself in. The desk where there should have been a policeman on duty was empty. She looked around for a bell or something to signal that she was inside, but there was none. Confused, Thea turned to the front door and saw Georgi trying to approach her, but Mrs. Mariola kept blocking his way. Finally, realizing that she could not hold him back, the teacher started calling for help. However, no one showed up.

'They were called urgently. Even the attendant left,' Georgi said, grinning brazenly. He had managed to reach Thea, took her by the hand, and tried to lead her through the front door. She fought back, but the man's grip grew stronger, and finally he managed to pull her towards him and guide her outside. Thea was defending herself, trying to hold on to something and not let him take her out into the street. Her hands gripped the doorframe tightly and resisted Georgi's efforts to move her away. Mrs. Mariola, for her part, had grabbed his jacket, trying to stop him. She continued to cry for help. Thea was also screaming and trying to free herself. In desperation, she shoved him roughly. Georgi cried out but continued to hold her tightly, perhaps hoping that someone from Thea's family would appear and help him. But no one was coming. The cries of Mrs. Mariola and Thea could be heard in the street, but no one came to help them either. Finally, the teacher let go of Georgi's jacket and, to his surprise, grabbed his hair. This forced him to free Thea. Seeing that he had lost the fight with the two women, he stepped out into the road, and Thea heard him yelling something into the phone.

After making sure Georgi would not return, the two women entered one of the closest rooms in the police station and blocked the door with a chair and a desk. Five minutes later, the policemen returned to the office, angered by the false report of an attempted murder they had received.

3

Thea watched from the room where they had hidden from the three police officers and wondered if she should trust them. For his illegal activity, Georgi paid many people to keep quiet. *He'd probably bought one of the three policemen too*, she thought.

'We have no choice,' whispered the teacher, who had sensed her hesitation and pressed the door handle. None of the officers paid attention to the opening door until they saw the two women standing in front of them. For a moment, the three of them were open-mouthed in surprise, then the policeman on duty, who had recovered first, gestured for them to stand in front of his desk. The other two stepped aside, watching them quizzically.

'Mrs. Mariola, why did you hide there?'

'They are chasing us, and we came here for help, but there was no one here.'

'Who was chasing you, and why didn't you wait in the waiting room?'

'Because they were trying to get us out of the precinct. This is Teodora Ivanova, my student.'

'We know each other,' said the policeman. 'We often have to visit her family. Who's after you?'

'My family,' Thea said quietly. Policeman Mirov looked at her in amazement. 'I gave birth to a girl yesterday afternoon. I named her Maria.'

'And why do you have to come to the police?' asked the other police officer named Popov.

'Because my family sold her.'

'They sold the baby?' Mirov was surprised.

'Yes, they sold her. Shortly after I gave birth to her, I saw my brother and father taking pictures of my daughter, then the father of my child came with a man and a woman, and they took my daughter away.'

The police officers looked at Thea and did not react. This was not what the two women expected.

'And what do you want us to do?' asked Popov.

'To find her.'

'Okay. We need the names of the child, date, and time of birth.'

'I gave birth to her at home. I don't have a birth certificate.'

'How are we going to look for her then?' asked Mirov.

Thea looked at him. He didn't trust her and wouldn't help her. She was overcome with despair; she didn't know how to prove that she wasn't making it up and that all this really happened.

'We can prove that she gave birth. By law, after birth, the child must be registered, regardless of whether it was born alive or stillborn,' Mrs. Mariola intervened.

'And how will you prove that she gave birth?'

'Get a medical team to examine Thea,' she said.

The three policemen stared at her.

'Okay,' Mirov said slowly. 'And what will that prove?'

'It will prove to you that she gave birth within the last twenty-four hours.'

'Probably Thea has already taken a shower and ...' Mirov tried to refuse.

'I haven't showered,' said Thea.

The policeman paused, looked at Thea again, and frowned. Then he looked away at the other two policemen. Neither of them said anything; they both looked in different directions. As the most senior officer in the hierarchy, he had to make the decision himself.

'Okay then,' he finally agreed. 'I'll call someone to examine Thea. But I can't open a case of a missing child without having information about it.'

'You can't or won't?' asked Mrs. Mariola in a teacher's tone, and this time Mirov froze.

'I can't, but Thea can write down what happened, and I can pass it on to the Regional Police Department.'

'Great!' said the teacher and looked invitingly at him. Mirov, who was her former student, got on the phone and called for a medical team to examine Thea. Then he invited Thea into one of the interrogation rooms and made her recount what had happened.

Three hours later, after a basic examination, many samples taken, urine and blood tests, the medical team confirmed that there had been a birth.

'A small part of the placenta was still inside her; we will examine it for the child's DNA, but I cannot guarantee the result,' said Doctor Lenov. He turned to Thea. 'I'm sorry for what happened.'

'When will the results be ready?' asked Mirov.

'No later than tomorrow. I will send all information to your email.'

'And you are sure that Thea gave birth recently?'

'Positive. I can't tell if the baby was born alive or stillborn, but there was definitely a birth.'

'Thank you, Doctor Lenov,' said Popov.

'Now what's next?' Thea asked.

'You will write in detail what happened, and I will send everything to the Regional Police Department. They work on cases like yours. I will need the names of everyone involved as well as a description of the couple who took the baby.'

'Maria.'

'What?'

'Her name is Maria.'

The officer nodded and handed her some blank sheets of paper and a pen. Thea began to write, and Mrs. Mariola continued to ask Mirov questions.

'How long will it take to find the child?'

'This case is different from others. As I already said, the Regional Police Department will take care of it.'

'Can you tell me who to look to for information?'

'No, I don't know who exactly will work on this case.'

Mrs. Mariola looked at Thea. She was one of her best students. Thea was special, but she didn't realise it.

'Can you protect her from her family? They will certainly want to bring her back to the hamlet.'

'Will she stay at your house?' asked Mirov.

'Yes. But I don't think we'll both be safe there. These people won't let her look for her daughter.'

'I can have the patrol car pass by your house over the next few days. At least until the results are out and the case is official.'

'Okay. After that?'

'My advice is to leave Bolengrad. The Woodpecker and his son will stop at nothing to find you.'

'The Woodpecker?'

'That's what we call her father at the police station.'

'I did not know that. Why do you call him Woodpecker?' asked Mrs. Mariola as fear started to seep into her expression.

'Trust me, Mrs. Mariola, it's better not to know,' said Mirov and turned his back on her.

Thea was writing intently, trying to remember everything that had happened yesterday. She didn't want to miss an important detail. She realized how important it was what she was going to write; even the smallest thing could lead to a clue to her daughter. At least that's what policeman Popov had explained to her. It took her two hours to finish her testimony, but finally, with trembling hands, she handed the papers to Mirov. He took them, looked at her, and nodded.

After spending almost, a whole day in a room with her, he had come to believe her story. Mirov had seen Thea several times while her family was being interrogated in the hamlet, but he had never spoken to her. At first, after hearing her story, he had decided that Thea was lying and somehow made the teacher believe her. But now he was sure that Thea had been through something terrible, and he was ready to do everything he could to help her. Mirov had been married for five years and had two children. The little child was a girl and the older a boy. Just the thought of someone taking them from him, or worse, selling them, made his heart skip a beat. You must be a freak to do that, he thought. And from what he found out; the father had made the deal. Mirov had never heard such a terrible story in his life. *Poor child*, he thought, staring into Thea's tired eyes.

'I will ask that this research be given priority,' he promised and called the patrol car to take Thea and Mrs. Mariola to the teacher's house.

A few minutes later, Mrs. Mariola and Thea entered the still-warm home and sat down on the sofa in the living room near the fireplace.

'We can't stay here long. Your family will come the moment they find the patrol has left the area.'

Thea nodded, then reached down and picked up the woollen blanket that had been left folded on the back of the sofa. She hugged it, curled up in a corner and stared at the fireplace in front of her. Thea no longer felt fear. Now all she felt was the cold. She needed to warm up, maybe then she would think more clearly.

Mrs. Mariola got up and helped her get more comfortable.

'Rest. I'm going to make something for dinner and call a few people. I might find someone to help us.'

'Thank you,' whispered Thea and almost immediately drifted off. The day's experiences had worn her out, and the warmth and calm voice of Mrs. Mariola made her relax. She closed her eyes, imagined that she was nursing her daughter again and fell asleep with a small smile on her face.

Mrs. Mariola left Thea to rest and entered the small kitchen. She took out some potatoes and other groceries from the fridge and started cooking. Cooking was her passion and the thing that helped her through difficult times. It was like therapy for her. Now, though, cooking wasn't helping her, and her hands were shaking with tension. Mrs. Mariola was convinced that soon Thea's family would come and force them out of the house one way or another. Bracing the doors and windows would not help them. She and Thea had to get out of here. Mariola was chopping the mushrooms and potatoes for the soup and wondering who to call. Who would shelter them at least for a few days until Thea got back on her feet? She couldn't call anyone in town; it had to be someone who lived far away and preferably in a bigger city, where Thea's family wouldn't be able to find them easily.

A soft cry coming from the sofa in the living room interrupted her thoughts, and she quickly went to see what was going on. Thea was having a nightmare and talking to someone in her sleep. Mrs. Mariola stroked her hair gently, and the young woman seemed to calm down. The nightmares would haunt her for a long time, the old woman thought. This was not the life she had imagined for

Thea. From the moment she met her, she had known that this child was special.

Thea looked a lot like her siblings. She had inherited her father's straight nose and her mother's big brown eyes with long eyelashes. There was no doubt that these were her parents. However much they looked alike, in everything else, Thea differed from her family. Mrs. Mariola remembered how when she found out that there was a child from the hamlet in the class she was supposed to lead, she was worried about how she would cope with this child. Thea's siblings were boisterous and difficult to control, and that was exactly what she expected from her. Instead of a wildly squealing child, however, there was a shy little girl standing in front of her. She had been fearful. She had looked nervously at her and the students in the classroom. Thea turned out to be an extremely smart and obedient student. Mrs. Mariola's problems did not come from her, *but because of her*. Her students hated Thea and insulted her at every possible opportunity. This often led to arguments with parents. The reputation of those living in the hamlet was not good, and it was difficult for Mrs. Mariola to explain that Thea was not one of them; she just lived there. But no one believed that about Thea. It took the teachers more than four years to integrate Thea with the other children. Her integration was not easy, but Thea eventually gained the respect of her classmates, yet this success was short-lived. Her relationship with Georgi quickly returned her to her previous position. Her love for this man got the best of her, or at least that's how Mrs. Mariola felt when she found out Thea was pregnant by him. For ten years, she had protected this girl, loved her as her own daughter, but that ended the moment Thea cut her out of her life. Now the teacher wondered if she could ever trust her again. *Maybe I should have. Love is blind*, she thought. She knew that from her personal experience.

Mrs. Mariola was watching the soup boil. She had taken a wooden spoon and was stirring the dark mixture. Then she realized that she was lost in her thoughts; she put the spoon down and moved into the living room. She pulled a chair closer to the sofa and stared at the woman sleeping there.

Thea had called her a few weeks before she gave birth. Of course, everyone in town was talking about her favourite student being pregnant, but Mrs. Mariola hadn't seen her with her own eyes and couldn't believe it. Until she received a strange call. Thea was crying and laughing at the same time.

'I'm going to be a mother,' she had told her. She had been excited but scared at the same time.

'Where will you live? With Georgi?'

'No. He doesn't want the baby. I will stay with my parents, at least at first.'

'Okay. If you need anything, call me,' she had said and hung up the phone in frustration. It wasn't the pregnancy that made her unhappy and offended, it was the way she was taught. Mrs. Mariola had offered her help then, but she hadn't expected that Thea would really need it. The two were very close, like mother and daughter. They had often talked about the young woman's future, and it included study programs and courses, but no plans for marriage. Now everything had changed. Mrs. Mariola would help her find her daughter, but the disappointment of Thea's actions still kept her on edge. Could she trust her? What if she helped her and Thea turned her back on her again? Mariola sighed and returned to the kitchen. She was just about to wake Thea up for dinner when the front doorbell rang. Thea startled and got up quickly from the sofa. The two women looked at each other in the living room, wondering what to do. Then, after hearing Mirov's voice through the door, they both relaxed, relieved.

'I came to check on you and bring some clothes for Thea to change into,' he said and handed a bag full of clothes to Thea. 'My wife had prepared them to give to the charity, but after I told her about you, she offered to bring them to you.'

'Thanks!' said Thea and headed to the bedroom to change.

'You can give me your old clothes as evidence,' shouted Mirov, then turned to his former teacher. 'I managed to contact the head of the Regional Police Department and tell him Thea's case. According to him, this is not the first time that the people from the hamlet have sold their babies. He suggested that you go with Thea to Sofia, and if she knows anything about it, she should testify. Do you think she knows anything about the other sold children?'

'Even if she knew before, she was afraid to speak. Can Thea be prosecuted if she didn't tell the police about it?'

'If she cooperates, they will probably record her as a witness and there will be no charges. However, if she does not cooperate and it is proven that she was there, there will be consequences, possibly a conviction.'

'I will talk to her about it. What will happen to her case?'

'It's hard to tell. It is best we to take you to the capital. There the people working in the Regional Police Department will explain to you what happens next. Tomorrow morning at eight I will come to pick you up. Is there someone you can stay with in Sofia?'

'As far as I know, she doesn't know anyone there, but I have acquaintances and I will contact them.'

'Okay. It would be good to warn them what they are going to get involved in,' said Mirov. He was about to say something else, but Thea's entrance into the room cut him off. She handed him the bag of her old clothes, and after thanking him again he left.

'What did he say?'

'Tomorrow morning, he will come to pick us up and take us to Sofia so that the Regional Police Department can begin to work on your case.'

'Will they find my daughter?'

'I don't know, Thea. We will talk to them tomorrow. They want to talk to you about something else, and I want you to think carefully and agree to help them.'

The two women were sitting down to dinner in the kitchen. Mrs. Mariola's words seemed to worry Thea. She pushed the bread and soup pan aside and prepared to get up from the chair.

'Sit down. You need to eat. We'll talk about it later.'

Thea hesitated briefly, then slowly began to eat. The warm food settled her stomach and made her relax. After they had dined, Mrs. Mariola resumed the conversation.

'I know that you are scared and that it will be difficult for you to talk about it, but I have to know. Do you know of any other trafficked children in your family or anyone else in the hamlet?'

Thea nodded.

'Did you attend the deals?'

'No. I only know what my mother and our neighbours told me. Two of my neighbours got pregnant by the wrong man, and after they gave birth, I never saw their babies.'

'Had they cheated on their husbands? Is that why they sold them?'

'Cheating is not an unusual thing in the hamlet. But when you already have five children from your husband, the sixth comes in addition, and when it is also from another man, it becomes even more unwanted.'

'Were you there when the babies were taken?'

'No. I'm not an eyewitness. This used to be arranged at the hospital. At least that's how I thought it was done.'

Thea spoke softly, her head bowed. She was ashamed to talk about it. She had always felt like her family was getting her involved in things she didn't want to be a part of or even want to know about. Now she was regretting that she hadn't gone to tell the police about all these things. She had buried her head in the sand, like an ostrich, and now the pass was coming back at her like a boomerang.

'God!' Mrs. Mariola exclaimed and got up from the chair. Thea knew what was going on in the hamlet and hadn't told anyone, not even her. 'But why were you silent?' asked the old woman, disappointment in her voice. 'Could you have at least told me?'

'I didn't want to involve you in this. The two women didn't want their babies; they were going to give them up for adoption anyway.'

'They sold them, Thea. They sold their own children.'

'Then I also thought it was good. What child would you wish to stay in this hamlet?'

Thea moved back to the sofa and began to cry. She curled up in one corner and buried her head in the small pillow. Mrs. Mariola didn't follow her this time and didn't try to calm her down. The shock hit her that her favourite student knew about this kind of trade and hadn't told anyone. She remained seated in the kitchen with her head in her hands. *At least she hadn't sold her own child,* Mariola thought.

A few minutes later, Thea had stopped crying. Her thoughts had returned to Maria and her plans to find her. Would Mrs. Mariola help her, she wondered. The teacher's frustration was obvious. She was still standing in the kitchen, and Thea could hear her breathing and sometimes sniffling, and she didn't know what to do. She wondered if she should go to her or let her calm down first. The last thing she wanted was to offend or upset Mrs. Mariola, but she couldn't turn back time. Thea had witnessed terrible things and she used to think it was better not to tell anyone about it. She now regretted that decision. If the people from the hamlet found out that she was willing to talk to the police about it, they would no longer be looking for her just to bring her back; they would try to kill her. The thought terrified her. Realizing what she had gotten herself into, Thea's blood seemed to freeze. Not only had she gotten herself into this, but so had the person who had always cared for her. If people from the hamlet found out what she had shared with Mrs. Mariola, the old woman would also be in danger. Thea got up and started pacing the room nervously. She had to get out of here as fast as possible.

'Mrs. Mariola,' she said as she entered the kitchen, 'you should not tell anyone what you know.'

'But why?'

'They will kill us. The moment they find out I'm going to talk to the police about it, they'll do everything possible to shut me up. If my family find out that you know something, they will hunt you down too.'

'But ...' Mrs. Mariola tried to protest.

'I know how much you care about me and how much you want to help me, and I am extremely grateful to you for that. But now I must leave immediately, and you must tell everyone that you fell asleep, and when you woke up, I was no longer here.'

'But Thea, where are you going?'

'I will go to Sofia to the Regional Police Department and tell them everything I know. This could help them find Maria.'

'But how are you going to get there? It's snowing outside again. They will find you. You won't be able to hide your tracks; there will be footsteps.'

'I have to take a chance. Either way, staying here until tomorrow morning is risky.'

'Even if you get there, where will you stay?'

'I don't know, but I have to get to Sofia. I'll come up with something.'

'In my opinion, it is better that you stay until the morning, and we go with the patrol car.'

'It will be late. Maybe someone from the police station will tell my dad that I'm going to testify against him. I am convinced that they will come here with my brother long before that. You must go somewhere else to spend the night, and I will go to Sofia.'

'But ...'

'Mrs. Mariola, my family is dangerous. I know them better than anyone. Think about where you might go. Somewhere where you won't be looked for and where you'll feel safe.'

'Boris will take me in,' Mrs. Mariola finally said, realizing that Thea was right.

'The physical education teacher. Isn't he married?'

'His wife died three years ago. A few months ago, Boris invited me on a date.'

'Okay. So, go to his house.'

'And you? Who will you go to?'

'I don't know, but we're not safe here anymore. Dress well and go.'

'Okay but promise me you'll call me when you arrive in Sofia. This is Boris's phone number.'

'I'll call you,' Thea promised, although she knew she wouldn't keep her promise. She helped the old woman to dress quickly and sent her through the garden gate. The P.E. teacher lived nearby, just two blocks away. Thea followed Mrs. Mariola until she saw her enter his home, then returned to the house, took a large handbag, and put some food and water in it. Then she looked around, saw a small picture of Mrs. Mariola, took it and put it in her back pocket. Who knew when she would see her patron again? Maybe it wouldn't be in this life, she thought, and left the house with tears in her eyes.

***

The distance between Bolengrad and Sofia was forty miles. Thea was sure it would take her at least twelve hours to walk there, and she knew there was only one way to get to the capital faster. She would go to the main road and hitch a ride. It was risky to stop cars at night, but she had done it many times before with her siblings and decided that the risk of running into a killer on the road was less than being found by someone from the hamlet. Thea knew exactly where to stand so she could see the cars coming, and over the years, she had learned which drivers would pick her up and which ones wouldn't. Drivers of more expensive cars avoided hitchhikers, and on a dark and snowy night like this, they would be even more careful. The blizzard continued, and Thea hoped someone would take pity on her and stop. She walked the path between Mrs. Mariola's house and the highway with her head down. To protect herself from the blizzard, she had taken a thick scarf and wrapped it around her head. By the time she reached the main road, the scarf was already wet from the snow and the cold was slowly starting to take over her body. Thea stood on the side of the road and raised her hand to the approaching cars. They all passed her by. People weren't very compassionate on this snowy night; no one stopped for her. Freezing, she hopped on the spot to warm herself in the snow.

After about half an hour of standing near the road, Thea finally saw a car pulling over. She crossed herself before walking to the car and prayed that the driver was a good person. As she approached the driver's window, her heart burst with worry as she recognized him. The driver was Bobby, one of Mrs. Mariola's private students. Thea and Bobby had often talked at school.

'Thea? Why are you out in this bad weather?' he asked and looked her over from head to toe.

'I have to go to Sofia. It's urgent.'

'Can't it wait until tomorrow?' Bobby said, and after he saw she was determined, he gestured to her to get into the car.

'Don't worry about me. I'll wait for someone else,' she said and started to pull away.

'I'll drive you. Get in the car. I can see you're already freezing.'

'No, Bobby, you better go. I don't want to involve you in this.'

'I'm already involved. I won't leave you alone out here in the cold. Are you getting in or not?' he asked, and she got into the car this time. After she settled into the seat next to him, Bobby drove off.

'What have you got yourself into?' he asked after a while.

'The less you know, the better.'

'Okay,' Bobby said and concentrated on driving.

Thea looked at him and regretted that she had agreed to let him drive her. She observed him as he drove. Bobby was a large young man; his short blond hair was always dishevelled, and his eyes were bright with the glint of inquisitiveness. Thea had rarely seen him worried. Bobby was one of the few who accepted her as an equal. He was a good man, and he was always very curious. She was convinced that he wouldn't leave her alone until she told him what was going on and why she was hitchhiking in this bad weather.

'I'm going to a party,' he said after a long silence. 'You can come with me if you want.'

'Thanks for the invitation, but I won't be able to come. I have other plans.'

'What are your plans?'

To go to the police, Thea almost said aloud. Instead, she just shrugged and said nothing.

'Is there someone to stay with?' he asked. 'A friend or relative? And which part of Sofia do you want me to take you to?'

'The central part, if it's convenient.'

'Where exactly in the central part?' Bobby continued to ask.

'I don't know,' she said, and that was the truth. She had not checked the whereabouts of the Regional Police Department office that had taken over the case. She only knew the name of the person who had taken over her case, which Mirov had told her shortly before he left.

'So, you don't know who you're going to?' Bobby asked. He waited for her to answer, but after she remained silent, he pulled into the gas station. 'I have to refuel.'

Thea nodded, but the gas station stop worried her. She didn't want other people to see her with Bobby in the car. Fortunately, there was only one other car parked there, and the people in it were complete strangers to her. Bobby was refuelling and looking at her. What was he thinking?

'I think you are running from something,' he said after getting back into the car. 'Are you running?'

Thea didn't answer right away. She hesitated about what to say to him, but she knew from his look that he already knew.

'I called my brother while I was paying the bill at the till. The rumour in the town is that the whole hamlet is looking for you.'

'That's right.'

'Are you in danger, Thea?'

'Yes.'

'You should have told me right away. That would have saved me stopping at the gas station.'

'Maybe I should have told you,' Thea whispered.

'Why are they looking for you?'

'It's better not to know.'

'Okay. And what is there in the central part of Sofia? Why do you want to go there?'

'I think that's where the Regional Police Department is dealing with ...' Thea stopped in time. She didn't have to tell him why she was going there.

'What are they dealing with?' Bobby asked.

'It's better not to know.'

'Okay,' Bobby said and handed her the cup of coffee he had bought for her. 'Take it – I think you need something to warm you up.'

'Thank you!' Thea said. Then she wrapped her hands around the warm cup of coffee and enjoyed the aroma wafting from it.

'You can stay with me until the morning,' he offered.

'I don't want to interfere with you, Bobby. If you want to help me, take me to the Regional Police Department.'

'You know there are at least ten, right? Where exactly is the one you want to go to? Do you have an address?'

'No, but whatever you take me to, they will know the person who works …'

'On your case. That's what you wanted to say, isn't?'

'Yes, but please stop asking questions.'

'I can't stop; it's in my nature. That's why I studied journalism.'

'Great –but in this case it's better not to know.'

'I'll find out – that's my job.'

Thea looked at him, and for the second time since she got in the car, she regretted agreeing to let him drive her.

'I can help you, Thea,' he insisted.

'You can't. The only thing that will help me is if you don't interfere and don't tell anyone that you picked me up.'

'Okay,' Bobby agreed, but Thea knew he wasn't going to stop. He was like that at school too, curious. *Good curious boy*, she added to herself and enjoyed the aroma of the coffee again.

An hour later, Bobby dropped her off at one of the police stations. He tried to go inside with her, but she stopped him.

'This is my phone number,' he told her and wrote it on a napkin that he got out of the car. 'Call me if you need help.'

'Thank you!' she said and hugged him. 'Please don't tell anyone you saw me today. It's for my own good and yours.'

'I promise. But you also have to promise me something.'

'Whatever you say.'

'If the story reaches the newspapers, I'll be the one you talk to.'

'I promise,' said Thea, and this time she was thinking of fulfilling her promise. Along the way, she'd decided that if the police couldn't help her find her daughter, she'd turn to the media, and Bobby had reminded her of that possibility. She waited for him to get into the car and drive off, then took a deep breath and entered the police station.

4

The police station where Bobby had dropped her off located in a big, old building. The door Thea came through was made of solid oak. It was heavy, and she had a hard time holding it open. When Thea walked inside, she looked around and saw two policemen sitting behind a large wooden desk. One of them looked at her and, seeing her confusion, motioned for her to come closer.

'How can I help you?' he asked.

Thea didn't answer right away. First, she took off her scarf, still wet from the snowstorm, and looked around. Apart from her, there were several other civilians in the office who were sitting on the side on old wooden chairs.

'Miss?' Again she heard the voice of the policeman and this time turned her attention to him.

'I'm looking for Lieutenant Koev from the Regional Police Department,' she said quietly.

'From which Regional Police Department?'

'I don't know.'

'Why are you looking for him?'

'It is a personal matter.'

'What is your name?'

'Teodora Ivanova.'

'Sit down please. I'll look for the lieutenant and let him know you're here.'

'Thank you,' said Thea and sat down on one of the wooden chairs. Even if she had not noticed from the outside that the building was old, everything inside spoke of it. The ceilings were high, the walls decorated, and oak furniture was predominant. Thea remembered a book she had read that described such old buildings in Sofia. Now she could feel the atmosphere and formality that permeated everywhere she looked. The doors were also taller than usual and beautifully carved. Thea looked around until her eyes landed on the people sitting in the chairs next to her. Two of them had many wounds on their heads, probably from a fight. Two of the women were wearing too little clothing for this cold weather, and Thea assumed they were in trouble with the law for the services they offered. A well-dressed man in his forties sat in the last chair. Thea wondered why he was here. The man felt her gaze and stared at her as well.

'Teodora Ivanova,' called the policeman on duty.

'Yes.'

'Would you come for a moment?'

Thea stood up, walked past the two women and the middle-aged man, and approached the desk.

'Lieutenant Koev knows nothing about your coming here. Your name means nothing to him.'

Thea was startled, about to say thank you and leave, but then turned back to the policeman.

'Maybe the name Thea will tell him something.'

'I'll ask him.'

'Thanks.'

The officer turned his back on her and started talking on the phone. Then he turned and handed her the phone.

'Hello,' she said nervously.

'What are you doing in Sofia? Mirov said he will bring you tomorrow morning. And why are you at this police station?'

'I didn't know where else to go.'

'And you decided just to come, ha?'

'I just ...'

'Wait for me there. In half an hour I will come to pick you up.'

Koev's voice was sleepy, and he had treated her roughly. The policeman had probably woken him up, and Thea's coming so unexpectedly had irritated him. She handed the phone back to the officer on duty, gave him a nervous smile, and went back to waiting in the wooden chair. While she had been on the phone, the two men and the two women had disappeared, and the only one left was the man in the beige coat.

'What did they bring you in for?' he asked after waiting for her to sit down. He had arrived after her, so he had no way of knowing she had come alone.

'For nothing,' she answered.

'Here everyone is in for something.' He smiled at her.

'What are you in for?' she asked.

'I am a lawyer. Do you need one?'

'No, I don't need a lawyer.'

'Are you sure?'

'Yes. I am.'

'Okay. You're the first person to sit in this chair here and not need a lawyer.'

'Are you looking for clients?' she asked.

'No. I've come to see one of my clients.'

'You see, I'm not the only one,' she said and turned her back on him.

However, the man did not give up. He approached her and whispered his name in her ear. 'If you need a lawyer, you can call me.'

'Thanks for the offer. I will keep it in mind,' Thea said and prayed that Koev would come soon and rid her of the nuisance.

Lieutenant Koev arrived an hour late. Thea had to listen to half an hour of the lawyer's stories and half an hour of the bragging of a former bodyguard. No one left her alone to get lost in her thoughts. When Lieutenant Koev entered, Thea recognized him immediately. He had come several times to the hamlet to question her family. She remembered that one time Koev wanted to talk to her too, but her brother pushed her inside the house and lied that she had gone somewhere.

'Thea?' the lieutenant called her.

'Yes,' she said, got up from the chair, and approached him.

'If my memory serves me right, we have already met,' he said and looked at her inquisitively.

'That's right.'

'Come with me. We'll go to my office.'

He took her lightly by the elbow and pushed her towards the front door. Thea tried to open it, but she was tired, and after the heavy door failed, Koev reached over and opened the door for her. Then he helped her into a small black car.

'Tell me, Thea, why are you here?' he asked her while driving.

'I understand you are inquiring about the children who were sold.'

'That's right. Besides your baby, we know of at least four more.'

'Four?' Thea was surprised.

'Yes. How many children do you know about?'

'Mine and two more.'

Koev said nothing and continued driving.

'Will you help me find my daughter?' Thea asked after a short silence.

'We will try.'

'I saw the people who took her,' said Thea, and tears flowed from her eyes. It had been more than a day since her daughter had been taken from her. These people could be almost anywhere.

'We will try to find them,' Koev said as he tried to calm her down.

Thea continued to cry. The tension of the last two days, as well as the pain she felt in her groin and legs, took their toll.

'I know you are tired, but we have to go to my office and talk there about your case and the cases of the other children.'

'Okay. I will do everything I can to help find them and find my daughter.'

Koev nodded and continued driving. The building he worked in was in one of the busiest business areas of the city, and only a few people knew its purpose. When Koev and Thea arrived, he helped her out of the car, then punched in the alarm code and opened the door for her. Thea went inside to find no one there. There were no attendants, no phones. The premises seemed unusable, and as she and the lieutenant climbed the stairs, their footsteps echoed. Thea was worried; she expected there to be more people, but all three floors they passed through were empty. There was no furniture or anything to suggest that this building was habitable until they reached the fourth floor. There it was as if they entered another world. There were at least fourteen desks in a large room with people working behind them. As soon as Thea and Koev walked in, they were greeted by a young blonde woman who wrote down Thea's name and date of birth, gave her a security bracelet to wear while in the building, and made her stand in front of the laptop to have her picture taken.

'What are on the other four floors?' Thea asked.

'Did you notice there are eight floors?' Koev was surprised. 'Mirov warned me that you are smart. Come, let's talk in my office.'

He led her past the desks and opened a glass door at the end of the hall. Thea thought that since Koev had a separate office, he was probably high up in the hierarchy. It wasn't a good sign, in her opinion. This meant that the crimes that had been committed in the hamlet were very important if a man like Lieutenant Koev had taken them.

'Sit down,' he told her and pointed to the chair in front of his desk.

Thea sat down and began to look around nervously.

'Relax, you are not in trouble at least for now,' he said and started taking out folders from one of the cabinets. Then he dropped the folders noisily on the desk. Thea jumped, her hands shaking.

'Do you see these files? These are files for sold children. Some of these kids you knew about, but you didn't do anything to save them, did you?' Koev pushed the folders towards her and made her open them.

'I didn't know,' she whispered softly.

'You knew!' He raised his voice. 'Of course, you knew. But you came to us only after your child was taken. It's a little late for that, isn't it?'

Thea didn't answer. This was not what she had expected from the lieutenant when he brought her here.

'You knew. The hamlet is small, there's no way a smart girl like you could have missed these deals,' he continued as he opened one of the folders. 'This baby died in the car last summer from suffocation. You probably knew about him but didn't do anything, and now you want everyone here to get down to business right now and find your daughter, who doesn't even have a name.'

Koev was screaming at her, and Thea was already shaking all over. Her legs bounced, and her knees hit the desk.

'I thought it was better for them,' she finally said, and tears flowed from her eyes again. 'They would have a better life than the one in the hamlet. Their mothers didn't want them.'

'Maybe your daughter will have a better life without you,' shouted Koev, and Thea covered her face with her hands.

'Please help me find her. Please!'

'We will help you if you help us,' said Koev and sat down in his chair. He looked at the young woman, who was shaking all over, and it seemed he felt that he had gone too far.

'If you tell us what you know, it might help us find her too. I need dates and names.'

'I know almost nothing,' said Thea, still with her hands in front of her face. 'Just rumours.'

'Then you will tell us what the rumours are,' said Koev in a calmer tone this time. He got up from the chair and approached her. 'This is the only way we will be able to help you and protect you from your family.'

'They will kill me – the moment I agree to talk to you they will look for a way to find me.'

'It's a little late, don't you think? You're already here talking to me. Nobody but me and you know what we're talking about.'

Thea saw he was right. Even if she didn't tell him what she knew, everyone would think she did.

'Now calm down. I'll ask Mary to bring you some tea, you'll take a little break, and then you'll tell me everything you know. Do you agree?'

'Yes.'

'Well then. Relax, you're safe here.'

Koev tapped her on the shoulder and then left the room. Thea stayed inside, still crying. Her whole face was covered in tears. Her cheeks were red, and her eyes were puffy. Thus, in despair, Mary found her.

'I brought you some tea to warm you up,' she said. When she got no answer, Mary tapped Thea on the shoulder to get her attention. Then she noticed blood dripping from the chair.

'You're bleeding! Come and lie down on the sofa. I'll call a doctor,' she said and helped her move. The few steps Thea took were followed by a trail of blood. The jeans she was wearing were drenched with blood between her legs.

'You've had a haemorrhage,' Mary said as she dialled the emergency number. Thea heard her speak, but she felt lost and very scared. She only calmed down when she saw a doctor next to her. Luckily for her, the urgent care centre was only a block away. The doctor examined Thea, gave her some pills, and asked Koev and Mary to let her rest for a day or two.

'There are two service apartments on the upper floor. We use them for cases like yours,' Mary said as she helped Thea to change and to settle into bed in one of the rooms upstairs. The moment Thea lay down, she fell asleep. Her sleep was not restful. She dreamed of blood, fighting, children who died of suffocation, and her daughter lying on a bed of cacti. When she woke up in the morning, she saw Koev standing by her bed.

'How do you feel?' he asked, placing his palm on her forehead to check her temperature.

'I'm fine,' Thea said, but her voice was weak and dry. It was hard for her to pronounce the words.

'I brought you breakfast. Do you think you can get up?'

'I will try.'

Thea rose from the bed and stepped onto the ground, swaying slightly. Seeing that she was unsteady, Koev helped her stand up better and escorted her to the table.

'Mary made you tea. The doctor said you will need to drink more fluids and eat well to recover.'

Thea looked at the table, which was strewn with various foods and fruits. She sipped her tea and thought that for the first time in her life, she didn't feel hungry. In the house where she lived until recently, food was scarce, and she ate only once a day. The sight of so much food should make her happy and whet her appetite, but for some reason, she didn't feel like eating. Koev saw her hesitation and pushed a bowl of fruit yogurt towards her.

'I eat yogurt when I don't feel hungry. It is quick to swallow, and at the same time it's healthy.'

Thea pulled the bowl to her and slowly began to eat.

'I would like to apologize to you for yesterday. I was wrong to be so rude to you. I had forgotten that you had recently given birth.'

'No problem. I'm used to being treated rudely by men.'

Koev nodded. Mary had told him how she had found Thea, and now he felt guilty and thought he was the cause of her emotional shock and possibly the haemorrhage.

'Last night, I never asked you how you managed to come to Sofia in this bad weather.'

'A friend of mine picked me up and dropped me off in front of the police station.'

'Does he know what you got yourself into?'

'Probably. According to him, everyone in the hamlet is looking for me.'

'He is right. They turned the hamlet and Bolengrad upside down. Your family found your teacher, but after they found out you left, they left her alone.'

'Did they hurt her?'

'Your father slapped her a few times, but she's fine.'

'Because of me, other people suffer,' said Thea and cried again. She felt helpless.

'You didn't do anything wrong, and they themselves offered you their help. But your family is another matter. I assume you were also mentally and physically abused while living with them.'

'Getting slapped was part of my job and something I'm used to, but when they hurt other people because of me, it hurts more.'

Thea's voice was still weak, and what she said at that moment affected Koev. The woman standing before him was not what he had expected. Not that Mirov hadn't warned him. He had told him that Thea was very different from her family, as if she had never been a part of them. Still, Koev had his reservations about her. Anyone involved in child trafficking, knowingly or not, was guilty in his view. The reasons were irrelevant. As much as Thea regretted it at that moment, he couldn't deny to himself the fact that she had known about these deals and kept quiet. However, he wanted to know the reason for her silence. Why hadn't she called? A person like her should know the difference between right and wrong.

While Koev drank his coffee and thought, Thea watched him. Koev was a handsome man, about forty years old, with a greying beard but still dark, curly hair. His forehead was often furrowed, and when he was worried, he would massage it with his fingers. His eyes were dark, almost black, and the glint in them as he spoke to her bothered her. Every time he looked at her, she felt like she was attached to a lie detector. His gaze pierced her, and she felt as if he was trying to look into her soul. But when he looked away, there was a gentle note in his eyes, and Thea could not explain this change. She had never met a man like him before.

'Today we will let you rest, but tomorrow I will have to question you,' Koev told her after drinking his coffee.

'No reason to wait – the sooner the better,' Thea said. 'I feel well now.'

'Are you sure?'

'Yes.'

'Okay. I'll prepare the paperwork and send Mary to pick you up. You try to eat something else. The doctor gave us a box of medicine. There are three compartments in the box with stacked pills for morning, noon, and night.'

'Thank you.'

Koev turned to her once more to make sure she was okay and then left the room. Once alone, Thea ate, took the pill that was left for the morning and stared out the window. Her arrival in Sofia had been sudden, and the traffic she saw on the street surprised her. The road was full of cars trying to get through. The drivers were nervous and honked their horns frequently. Thea looked around at the other buildings and found that most of them were new and there was a lot of construction going on. In the distance, she could see the mountain, which was white with snow.

'Good morning,' she heard Mary say. 'Koev told me that you feel well, and you want to conduct the interview. I didn't believe him, but now that I see you sitting up straight, I know he didn't lie to me. Would you like more tea or coffee?'

'No, thanks. Maybe just a glass of water.'

Mary poured her water into a glass she took from the kitchen and returned to Thea, who was still watching what was happening through the window.

'The traffic is terrible in the morning. Welcome to the urban jungle.'

Thea smiled slightly. 'I have never been to Sofia before,' she said quietly.

'All capital cities look alike. Lots of traffic and nervous drivers. As well as the more pleasant sights – museums, galleries, and places that are attractive to tourists.'

'I wish I had come here as a tourist.'

'Trust me, I feel that way too sometimes. How old are you?'

'I will turn nineteen in April.'

'You look and talk like an older person.'

'I had to grow up fast. I thought I was smart and different, but now I feel like the biggest fool in the world. I let them take my baby. In fact, I let them sell her.'

'We will find her.' Mary tried to calm her down.

'I hope so. This is another day without her. Do you have children, Mary?'

'No, but I hope someday I will.'

'When you give birth to your first child, you will understand. Even though I only saw my daughter for a little while, I can't tell you how much I miss her now.'

Mary didn't know what to say. She could feel Thea's anguish. The only thing she hoped for was to never experience that feeling of helplessness that carried this young woman. 'Let's go downstairs,' she suggested and headed for the front door. Thea followed with her head bowed.

The room they entered was different. It only had a microphone in it, and although Thea couldn't see any cameras around, she was sure there were. They just weren't in plain sight.

'How do you feel?' Koev asked her.

'Better.'

'Are you sure you are ready to talk to us?'

'Yes.'

'Okay. Let's start with your names. What is your name?'

'Teodora Vasileva Ivanova, but everyone calls me Thea.'

'Why are you called Thea? Is there an incident or something that your nickname is associated with?'

'A few hours before I was born, my mother watched a movie in which the main character was called Thea. She wanted to give me this name officially, but my grandmother, my father's mother, did not agree, so they decided to call me

Teodora. Nevertheless, my mother called me Thea, and in the end, it stayed that way. Very few people in the hamlet know my real name.'

'Okay,' said Koev and got up from the chair. He had a pen in his hands and was rolling it between his palms. 'What can you tell us about Georgi? How did you meet?'

Thea shifted nervously in her chair. She hadn't expected to be asked about him. 'He comes to the hamlet often.'

'Can you remember when you first saw him?'

'I think a few years ago, but I'm not sure.'

'And who was Georgi talking to in the hamlet?'

'With everyone. Sometimes we all gathered in the street to eat and be merry. You know what I mean. We played music, ate, and danced. He often came to these celebrations. Sometimes we got together for an occasion – a occasion – a wedding, an engagement, or the birth of a child. Now that I think about it, almost every time he was there.'

'And who did he talk to?' Koev asked again.

'I told you, he talked to everyone.'

'Think, Thea. There must be someone working for him. I'm guessing it's a man, but it could be also a woman.'

'My brother Rado,' she whispered after a short thought. 'Those two are very close.'

The thought that her brother had known from the beginning what would happen to her baby horrified her. Thea and Rado had been very close when they were children. Then he got married and everything changed. Another soul seemed to have taken up residence in his body. He had become a man who smiled on the outside but seethed with malice on the inside. Thea had to admit, however, that if any other woman had been as rough with him as she had been after giving birth, she would have been bruised and covered in wounds. The fact was that Rado had hit her several times, but not with all the force he used when he hit his wife.

'You said that you first saw Georgi a few years ago. What happened after he first came? Was there an incident, something that made an impression on you?'

'No, I do not think so. I think I first saw him at my sister Yana's wedding. She then moved to live in a village near Sofia.'

'Have you seen your sister recently?'

'Yes, shortly before I gave birth, she came with her husband and children. Yana has two children.'

'What is her husband's name?'

'Ivo.'

Koev motioned to Mary and asked her to bring him a tablet.

'Now I'll show you a picture. I want you to tell me if you know this man.'

Thea nodded and waited for Mary to return. The room was quiet for a moment, then Mary came in and showed her the picture on the tablet.

'I do not know this man. I've never seen him.'

'Okay. His name is also Ivo, and I wanted to make sure we were talking about different people. Tell me about Georgi. How did it happen that he is the father of your child?'

Thea swallowed before answering and sipping from the glass of water left on the table in front of her. She was uncomfortable talking about her intimate life.

'As I already mentioned, Georgi often came to the hamlet. Sometimes he stopped by the house and drank with my father until late at night.'

'He was courting you.'

'Perhaps. I liked him very much. I guess he sensed that and took advantage.'

'Don't be hard on yourself,' Mary intervened. 'I saw your pictures from before you finished school. You were very beautiful, and you still are.'

'Probably. And stupid,' Thea said sadly. 'Georgi started coming more and more often. Once he took my hand, took me behind the house, told me I was beautiful and kissed me. And so, it all began.'

'Where did you meet?' asked Koev.

Thea was silent for a while. The pieces of the puzzle were falling into place before her eyes, and she couldn't believe how blind she had been.

'He always came when there was no one in the house. He would spend a few hours with me and then leave.'

'So, you haven't been to his house?'

'Never.'

'Do you know where he lives?'

'Yes. My teacher, Mrs. Mariola, had asked the school security to check where he lives.'

'You mean Mrs. Mariola Purr.'

'Yes. Everyone calls her Mrs. Mariola. At the beginning of her career, students made fun of her last name and the school management decided to introduce her only by her first name.'

'Okay. So, you've never been in Georgi's house?'

'No. He didn't want us to go to Bolengrad. He kept saying he couldn't wait...' Thea did not continue. Tears streamed down her cheeks.

'I know it's hard, but we have to continue,' Koev said and nodded to Mary.

'I'll get her some mint tea. It might calm her down.'

'Don't worry. I'm fine,' Thea said. Then she dried her tears, took a deep breath, and looked at Koev. 'If you want to know where Georgi lives, you can ask Mrs. Mariola.'

'We know where he lives, but we were wondering if you entered his house. Although I know he hardly wanted to risk you meeting his wife.'

'His wife? So, she was right all along.'

'Who?'

'Mrs. Mariola. After I told her about Georgi, she called me and warned me that he was married, but I didn't believe her.'

'Yes, I'm sorry you have to hear this, but he has a big family. I'm surprised you didn't know. Bolengrad is a small town, you only had to ask few people, and you would have found out.'

'I should have asked. Do you think our child was planned?'

'On the contrary. I don't think the pregnancy was planned. We assume that your family owed him money and paid off their debt through you. Georgi likes young girls but rarely stays with them for more than a week or two. However, he has been with you for almost a year.'

"What we think is,' interrupted Mary, 'that Georgi has feelings for you.'

'This is not possible. He sold our child.'

'Men like him don't have strong feelings for their children. He does not care for his children at all; he has not even given them his name.'

'What? You said he is married.'

'He has been living with his wife for more than fifteen years, but he has never married her. They have children, but they all bear her surname. In our opinion, Georgi sees children as competition. He pays attention to the mother, sometimes takes her to a restaurant, but ignores the kids.'

Thea opened her mouth to ask something, but the shock of what she heard stopped her.

'I know it is difficult to understand,' said Koev. 'But we think that Georgi is at the heart of child trafficking. The problem is that we don't know who his contact is, and we have no information about how the deal is done. Georgi doesn't have a computer or laptop. The only device he uses is the phone. He's obviously calling someone, but we have no way of knowing who. We tried to make a fake deal with him, but he felt it. He's crazy and doesn't trust anyone.'

'And if I give you his phone number, can you find out who he's talking to?'

'He doesn't talk on his personal phone. Every month we request a printout of the calls from his mobile phone operator. There is nothing suspicious. There must be a second phone, but so far, we have no proof of that. Have you seen him talking on two different phones?'

'No. In fact, he hardly ever used his phone when he came to see me.'

Thea's face flushed at the memory of his visits.

'What can you tell us about children who were sold from the hamlet?' asked Koev.

'I know of two babies that were born, but then I never saw them. When I asked the mothers where they were, they told me that they had given them up for adoption. My brother once got drunk and told me they took good money for them. I also heard my mother and the neighbours talking about it.'

'So, you really don't know anything specific?'

'No, as I told you, I only know rumours. I haven't seen who took them and when.'

Koev sat down in the chair and sighed heavily. 'Then we have nothing against them,' he said.

'And what about the family I saw taking Maria?'

'We are looking for them, but so far there is no result.'

Thea strained to remember anything else but couldn't.

Koev got up from the chair and looked out the window. Thea wondered what he was thinking. Had he believed her? Hardly. She could see the tic on his cheekbone, which gave away that he was nervous. He tapped his hand on the sill for a while, probably not even realizing what he was doing, until at one point he turned to Thea. 'There is one way that you can help us, but it is risky.'

'No, you won't use her,' protested Mary. The blonde got up from the chair and headed towards him. He stopped her with a gesture and motioned for her to return to her seat.

'Her daughter's trail is getting colder by every minute. Let's let her decide whether or not to risk it.'

'Whatever it is, I'll do it, as long as it takes me to her.'

'You won't like it,' warned Mary, 'and you should know that I am against it.'

'What can I do?' Thea asked, looking at Koev.

'Return to the hamlet,' he said. Thea looked at him in astonishment.

'Only your friend Bobby knows you're here, and I'll make sure he doesn't tell anyone. You can go home with a curled tail and trick Georgi again. That's the only way we'll find out who his connection is.'

'I'm sorry, but I can't do it.'

'You can,' insisted Koev. 'I have been working on this case for eight years. I did everything I can, but so far, I have no trace. We need an insider; someone we can trust. We have nothing against Georgi, and the chance of finding your daughter and the other children is almost zero if you don't help us.'

Thea looked at Mary.

'I already told you that I am against it, but the decision is yours.'

'I'll let you think,' Koev said, 'but you have to hurry. If you decide to help us, every minute you're away from the hamlet takes you away from the opportunity to return there.'

'So, you won't help me find Maria?' she asked.

'Even if I wanted to, I have no information about where she was taken. The only person who knows where she is is her father, Georgi.'

Thea exchanged glances with the man in front of her. Then Koev turned his back on her and looked out of the window. The blonde joined him. They were giving her time to think about the offer he had made. Thea looked at the folders in front of her, then her gaze returned to the lieutenant. His right hand was still holding the pen, and his fingers were so dug into it, as if they were going to break it at any moment. Koev was nervous, Thea was sure of that, and for her there was no longer any doubt that his proposal was serious and not some trick. She took a deep breath.

'Okay. I will do it,' she said, her voice trembling with tension.

Koev and Mary turned to her almost simultaneously.

'Thea, you don't have to answer right away,' the blonde warned her.

'You don't understand. I can't let them take Maria faraway. I will do everything I can to find her as soon as possible.'

'They may not believe your story and kill you,' said Mary. 'I want you to think twice.'

'I will take the risk.'

Mary looked sullenly at Koev. There was a great tension in the silent room. Thea was rubbing her palms together nervously, and Koev had the pen in his left hand and was tapping the desk with it. That was the only sound that could be heard.

Mary watched the lieutenant and Thea and seemed to wonder what they were thinking. Finally, Koev looked at Mary questioningly. He was obviously waiting to hear what she had decided.

'Okay. Let's prepare you for your return,' Mary said, turning to Thea before leaving the room.

5

Half an hour later, Mary led Thea into another room that had lots of packed stuff. She pulled out one of the labelled boxes, opened it, and handed Thea her old clothes.

'Put them on. You must return to the hamlet with them.'

Thea changed her clothes, and the smell of blood and sweat wafted over her immediately.

'You will tell them that you took a quick shower at Mrs. Mariola's.'

'Okay. And where was I the rest of the time?'

'Koev will tell you what story you will tell your family. He and our colleagues are currently planning it. But you have to be persuasive. Also, you have to do everything possible for Georgi to come back to you. You know what that means, right?'

'Yes, I must be his lover again.'

Thea frowned just at the thought of being with him again, but she tried not to think about it now.

'I hope you understand that it may take time until Georgi trusts you again. Probably months or even a year. Don't pressure him, don't ask him questions. You have to get him to talk to you about it. People like him are very cautious and unpredictable. One wrong word and he's gone forever.'

'How will I know what he's doing if I don't ask him questions?'

'Just observe what is happening around you. As Koev already mentioned, we think Georgi has a second phone, through which he arranges his meetings. Try to find out if he uses it while he's in the hamlet. Also, while you're there, find out who he talks to, and who does he take time to talk to alone. Thea, what we didn't tell you is that we're pretty sure your cousin Benny is pregnant by the wrong man, and there's probably going to be a new deal soon. Listen, but don't question.'

'And how will I contact you?'

'We will send a courier every week.'

'Couriers don't come to the hamlet.'

'Your brother has started ordering things online. For two weeks, a courier has been coming and leaving the parcels at the first house. A little further down there is an old well. You can leave the information there, but you have to be careful. We'll leave you devices to tell us what you've learned.'

'Okay,' Thea agreed, and the two women left the room and headed to Koev's office. When they entered, Thea noticed that there were three other people in the room besides him.

'You have to sign an agreement,' said one of them and explained to her all the clauses in the agreement. After Thea read and signed the papers, he left the room.

'Leave us alone,' said Koev, and after the others had left, he stared at her.

'I want to clarify something before you leave,' he said and looked at one corner of the room. Then he turned his head and looked her straight in the eyes. 'I don't want you to go back there.'

Thea was surprised by what he said, she opened her mouth to say something, but he stopped her.

'What I want to tell you is that you and I both have no other choice. You want to find your daughter, and I, apart from finding her, want to find the other children and stop the people involved in this trafficking. I want to ask you to be careful and the moment you feel your life is in danger to find a way to tell us. Please stay alive. Don't do anything risky. Do we understand each other?'

'Yes,' Thea said, still surprised by what he said. Then she rose from the chair, but he motioned for her to sit down again.

'We will try to put a camera on the old well. The camera will have a motion sensor and every time someone approaches, I will receive a personal message. If you ever feel threatened, go there first, and give a signal, something only you and I will know. For example, some atypical gesture for you. Put your hands over your nose for a short while as if you're going to sneeze at any moment. Can you do it?'

Thea raised her hands to her nose, and to her surprise, almost sneezed.

'Yes, you can instinctively sneeze. Do you have any questions?'

'Yes. The dead child in the car … when did it happen?'

'Last May. We found the car abandoned in front of the entrance of a block. Whoever left the baby wanted us to find it quickly. We assume they were the people who took the child.'

'Last May, Bonka gave birth to a boy,' Thea said softly, her voice trembling. 'What if Maria …' She couldn't finish the question.

'We will continue to look for the people who took her. This is the first time we have an eyewitness account, so the likelihood of finding them is greater. However, we are not sure if they are just the transport. In human trafficking, the seller and buyer rarely meet in person. In most cases, they pay couriers, people who deliver the so-called "shipment".'

Thea's face paled. The information Koev was giving her was more than she could emotionally handle. 'But that means we don't know who will take care of her.'

'I'm sorry, Thea. I know what I said shocked you, but it's better to know what you're dealing with. What my team is suggesting is that maybe Georgi will use these people again. Finding another couple that moves the kids won't be easy for him. I think he has been using them for years. We received a similar description eight years ago when we found out about the first sold child.'

'How did you find out about it?'

'By chance. The new parents had withdrawn a large sum of money a few months after being denied an adoption and a finance colleague had become suspicious. They had withdrawn fifty thousand euros. The bank branch they had requested the cash from did not have this money and made a request to the main office. That's how we knew something was wrong. Unfortunately, we found the couple after the baby had already been handed over by the couriers. The child's number on his hand from the maternity ward was still there, so we knew who the mother was. Since then, all other children we know of have been born in a home environment.'

'Eight years ago?'

'Yes.'

'And it was from the family in the hamlet, so it's eight years old now.'

'Yes. I'm sure you know who the kid is and what its name is.'

'Yes,' said Thea and looked sadly at Koev. 'This child would probably be better off with his new parents.'

'Probably,' agreed Koev. 'But if these people have been refused to adopt a child several times, then there is something wrong with them, don't you think?'

Thea didn't answer. She had always thought that anywhere, but the hamlet was a better place for a child to live.

'Thea, I will take you as close as possible, and we will refine your story along the way. Now go get something to eat and drink. I'll come and pick you up in ten minutes.'

'Okay,' she said, slowly getting up from her chair and leaving the office. Just before she closed the door, she heard Koev's heavy sigh. The moment she came out Mary saw her and led her to the small kitchen upstairs. Thea quickly ate a sandwich, drank the warm coffee Mary had made her, and took two of the pills the doctor had prescribed.

'You can take the pills with you. The name of the doctor who examined you in Bolengrad will be written on them. I imagine your relatives know about this examination and they will not be happy that you allowed them to examine you. We will spread the word in Bolengrad that they found no proof that you were pregnant. In my opinion, Georgi will not take this bait, but Koev thinks that if you manage to convince your family and if you seem desperate enough, eventually he will believe it too.

Thea shuddered at the thought of having to go back there, but she had no choice. Even if she didn't go back to her parents' house, she had nowhere to go, and the likelihood of her finding Maria on her own was very slim.

A few minutes later, Koev picked her up. This time they used the elevator to the underground car park. Thea could smell the heavy smell coming from her clothes. It reminded her of the birth and everything that happened just two days ago. Koev was walking in front of her, but when he arrived at the car, he waited for her and helped her sit on the seat. While driving he told Thea what to say and what to do to make her story convincing. He had taken a spray bottle, filled it with water, and when they got close to the hamlet, he sprayed her hair until it was wet, as if she had been outside for a long time. The cold water immediately made her shiver.

'Great,' Koev told her, satisfied with the desired effect. 'Remember, at the slightest danger, run to the old well and give me a sign. The technicians will put the camera on tonight. I guess everyone will be busy talking to you, and we will have plenty of time to do so. There will be information for you, which will be placed in a stone marked with rust. As soon as possible, first check what is there.'

Thea nodded and continued to shiver from the cold.

'Now go before you catch a cold. And take care,' Koev told her. Then he hugged her for courage and got back in the car. On the way to the capital, Koev wondered if he would see her again. He hoped he had made the right decision and that he wouldn't regret it.

At the same time, Thea was walking down the road to the hamlet. Koev had left her two miles away. He had told her to drag her feet to absorb the mud on the slushy road. The lieutenant had deliberately scratched her palms, lightly enough to leave marks, and had advised her to cry as she went to achieve the desperate look, they wanted her to achieve. Thea took his advice and cried, gave vent to her feelings with all her soul. She cried for her baby and for her fate. *Who deserves such a fate?* she wondered, and the thought made her tears well up even more. When she approached the first house and her neighbour Ivan saw her, he barely recognized her. Thea pulled him close, grabbed him by the sleeve of his winter jacket, and continued to sob. He first took her hand, then realizing who she was, slapped her hard with his free hand.

'Bitch. How dare you come back here?' Ivan said and released the sleeve of his jacket from her hand. 'Rado, the harlot is back.'

Ivan shouted once more, and the people of the whole hamlet came out into the street. Men, women, and children watched Thea and waited to see what her brother and father would do. The two men approached her, and as everyone expected, they started hitting her. First with slaps, and after her body fell to the ground, they continued with kicks. Thea cried and screamed for help, then began to beg them to forgive her. After deciding she had been hit enough, her brother and her father walked away and left her lying on the ground. Thea writhed in pain, but no one helped her. Her father and Rado had not spared her, but they did not kill her; they did not take sops or stones. She would survive, she thought, and began to pray. Little by little, people started to go home, and finally only she and her family remained on the street.

'What are we going to do with her?' Rado asked.

'Get her inside the house. We have to find out what she told the police,' her father growled. Rado moved closer to her, and Thea tried to stand up but fell back into the mud. Her head was dizzy from the blows her father had inflicted on her, and she was never able to get up. Rado called their neighbour, and they both carried her to her native house. *I survived*, she thought, and then passed out.

***

When she woke up, it was already night, and from the sounds, Thea guessed it was around midnight. She looked around and saw that they had tied her to a chair in the kitchen. Muffled voices drifted from the living room. Even if she didn't hear Georgi's voice, the smell of his aftershave told her that he was in the house. Perhaps he and her family were deciding her fate now, she thought and began to pray. She prayed for herself and her child. For Maria not to follow the fate of the baby who died in the car. She prayed to be spared and to find a way to her and get her back. Then she stopped praying and listened to the conversation in the other room. Rado and Georgi were arguing about something; it was not related to her, but about money. After a brief conflict, they reconciled, and her brother offered to bring more beer. When he entered the kitchen, Rado noticed that she was conscious but said nothing. He walked past her, grabbed two beers, and returned to the living room. He gave her more time to recover. How could he beat her until she passed out and then feel sorry for her, she wondered, and thought again that two different souls lived in her brother's body. *Good and evil in one body,* she said to herself, then wearily laid her head down and fell asleep. The painkillers she had taken at Mary's office had eased her pain.

When she awoke again, Thea found that the conversations in the next room had stopped. Silence had enveloped not only their house but the entire hamlet, and even the ever-barking dogs had fallen asleep. She tried to get up, but her father and brother had tied her up well. Cold air was blowing from the window, whose joinery had come off, and Thea could feel the draught in her bones. She was cold, but the thought that she had survived warmed her. They had taken pity on her, she was glad, and tried to go back to sleep. But the cold kept her awake for a long time. The painkillers had also worn off, and Thea began to feel pain almost everywhere in her frozen body. Her hands, feet, and lips were trembling.

She tried to move and warm herself, but she couldn't move at all. All attempts to free herself were unsuccessful, so finally, exhausted by the effort, she stared at the moon. As a child, she often looked at this glowing satellite and dreamed of seeing new places and new worlds. This was obviously not going to happen, she reminded herself, and then decided that her dreams had already changed drastically. Her desires for adventure were replaced by her desire to hug her baby again. Thea wanted nothing more than to find her and bring her back. And the people who could help her and tell her where she was were the same people who separated her from Maria. She had to find a way and make her family trust her again. With that thought, Thea laid her head down on her chest, began counting sheep, and finally fell asleep.

A dog barking woke her up. It was getting dark, and the clattering of kitchen utensils could be heard from the neighbouring houses. The women had risen to make breakfast for the children and coffee for the men. There were about thirty houses in the hamlet, in which about forty families lived. The house where Thea's family lived was one of the oldest on the street. Her grandfather had built it shortly before her father was born and bequeathed it to him before he died. Thea's grandfather was considered the founder of the hamlet, and for many years he had led it as mayor, although he did not officially hold such a position. After his death, Thea's father took charge of the settlement. Every change, every piece of news in the community was shared with him. Although her family were wealthy, they actually owned the least amount of land, and their house was one of the smallest. They didn't even have a car. The only vehicle was her brother's old motorbike. *Where did all the money go?* Thea began to wonder now. The other families paid a kind of tax to her father, which, according to her accounts, was a considerable monthly sum. However, there was often nothing to eat in the house, and the scandals between her mother and father became more and more frequent and violent. Her brother, who had moved three houses up, often came over to help Thea get her parents out of yet another scandal, which always ended with her mother having a black eye.

Thea wondered where her mother was now. She hadn't seen her when she arrived yesterday either. Thea listened to hear what people were talking about as they passed the house, but most weren't talking; she could only hear their footsteps. Others talked about trivial matters. Thea realized that everyone was probably being cautious and didn't want to comment on her appearance, not on the street. As she listened, she heard her brother's voice cursing softly. Then the front door opened, and she heard him enter. Rado knocked loudly on the bedroom door, and after hearing swearing on the other side of the door, entered the kitchen. Thea raised her head and tried to meet his eyes. She wanted to know what mood her brother was in, but Rado looked away, poured water into the coffeemaker, and took coffee from the only cupboard in the kitchen. After the coffee was ready, he poured two large glasses of the dark liquid, took them, and left the kitchen without looking at Thea. He would wake her father and then talk to her. Apparently, the interrogation that was supposed to take place yesterday was going to take place this morning, she thought and swallowed hard. Her fate was not yet decided. Everything now depended on her and how convincing she would be. Fear gripped her again, and this time Thea's lips and hands did not tremble from the cold. Panic gripped her, and her heart beat faster than usual. Thus, completely desperate, her brother and father found her. Rado untied her hands, and her body drifted slightly forward. Instead of supporting her, however, her brother moved away, which gave her father a chance to get closer, and, recoiling from the slap he gave her, Thea's head rolled to the right and her back rested against the back of the chair.

'Don't you dare cry again. No matter how much you cry and scream, no one will help you,' he said, taking a step back and picking up the cup of coffee he had left on the small kitchen counter. 'What did you tell the police?'

Thea glared at him. At that moment, she hated her father more than ever.

'I told them everything. Absolutely everything, but they didn't believe me.'

'You're lying,' her father said quietly through gritted teeth, put the cup down again, and approached her. Instead of hitting her, however, he leaned towards her ear. 'I don't believe you. I know they sent you to Sofia. You've been gone all day, so don't kid me. Tell me the truth.'

'I'm telling you the truth,' Thea whispered, frightened by the tone with which her father spoke to her.

'No, you're not telling me everything. But the teacher must know. Someday she'll be back at her house, and we'll find out what you told her.'

'And she didn't believe me. The doctor said there was no proof I had given birth and she thought I was lying to her. She kicked me out of her house.'

'I don't believe you!' shouted her father. 'Do you believe her, Rado?'

'No.' Her brother shook his head. 'Not at all. Her hair smelled like a nice shampoo when I saw her on the road yesterday.'

'I took a quick shower at Mrs. Mariola's house. That's why I couldn't prove that I gave birth.'

'You're lying!' shouted her brother this time. 'You're lying! Why did you come back?'

'Rado,' she cried and hoped to give as convincing a look as possible, 'you are my family. Where else should I go?'

'Where? At the *lady's* house. Didn't she promise to help you, to shelter you?' said her brother mockingly. 'You can see now how the educated people keep their promises? They don't care about you at all.'

Thea continued to cry as her brother and father watched her. Then they asked her the same questions again and again in order to confuse her. Although they had not finished school, they were both smart and knew how to pressure and manipulate people. The interrogation they conducted lasted three hours. Thea kept repeating the same thing, and finally they seemed to believe her. They untied her legs and made her go to the bedroom. The moment she got in there, they locked the door. A little later, Thea heard her mother coming home and cooking in the kitchen. Rado had left the house, and her father was probably sitting cross-legged on the couch watching TV. This was the normal family atmosphere on weekdays.

Thea wondered where her mother had been. Her absence from the house for so long was unusual. Her father was very jealous and did not allow her mother to roam the streets alone for a long time. Thea looked out the window and saw that the bench usually occupied by neighbours was empty this time. There seemed to be tension in the hamlet. She thought not everyone would have agreed with her father and brother's decision to spare her. This would surely bring trouble to her family, but Thea didn't want to think about that now. The only thing that concerned her at the moment was to find out as quickly as possible where her daughter was and who Georgi's connection was. And just as she thought about him, he appeared at the door. Lost in thought or distracted by the pain, Thea hadn't even realized he had entered the house.

Georgi stood next to her on the bed and began to examine her from head to toe.

'Look what they did to you,' he said and tried to stroke her hair. Thea instinctively raised her hand and pushed his hand away. Then she remembered that the goal was to calm him down and gave him a small smile.

'Please, don't touch me. I'm dirty. Let me take a shower first,' she said quietly.

'So, you're not mad at me?' he asked, looking into her face quizzically. He was testing her, she thought.

'On the contrary. What father sells his child?' she said reproachfully and looked at him angrily.

'You're mad, but you'll be fine. She'd be better off somewhere else, don't you think?'

He reached down to stroke her hair again and this time she didn't push him away, but she still glared at him.

'You are beautiful,' Georgi said. 'And you're right, you need to shower and change.'

He looked at her once more, turned his back on her, and left the room. However, he did not forget to lock the door. Thea breathed a sigh of relief. She hoped she had been persuasive, and he believed her. She heard her father and Georgi talking, but no matter how hard she tried, she couldn't hear exactly what they were saying. Then the door opened, and her mother came in with a bowl in hand.

Thea's mother's name was Kina, but everyone called her the mayor's wife. Only her husband called her by name. Kina was a plump woman with beautiful black hair, large brown eyes, and a cute nose. Everyone talked about how she used to be the most beautiful woman in the area, but now that beauty seemed to have washed away. Her eyes were sad, her lips were set in a frown, and her gait was slow, heavy, as if she were carrying a mountain on her shoulders. Thea remembered how when she was little, her mother would often sing at the village gatherings. However, her songs had stopped after a while, and the cheerfulness that radiated from her years ago was now gone. Thea also remembered that when she was little, her mother had often protected her. Then something changed, and there was a coldness between them. That's what Thea felt now. A chill that could not be warmed by the warm soup her mother brought. Kina stood next to her daughter and handed her the bowl. She stared at Thea briefly, then turned her back on her and left the room. This time the door remained unlocked.

It took Thea two weeks to recover from her wounds. During this time, her family kept her locked in the house. Her duties were to cook, clean and keep quiet. Georgi came every few days, but he was never alone with her. Still, she could feel his gaze. He followed her every move and often stared into her eyes as if trying to understand what she was thinking. On these occasions she would sometimes frown, other times she would smile slightly. Mary had told her that her behaviour would confuse him and keep him interested in her.

'In any case, do not give in to him easily. Men like him love the challenge; they love the game. They are hunters, and you are the trophy. So, you have to convince him that he is worth playing for you. But don't overdo it because it will show. A little smile, a little sadness, and sometimes tears. If that doesn't help, you'll have to apply the seduction game. A slight baring of the shoulder and a garment to emphasize your waist. But this will only be a last resort.

Either way, you have to wait for your belly to shrink after giving birth. If you try to seduce him visibly, he will quickly get bored of you.'

'What if he doesn't like me anymore?'

'You will come up with something to get his attention in another way. But I think he has a crush on you.'

'I hope so,' Thea had said then, but now, returning to this conversation, she realized how right Mary was. The slight smile she gave to Georgi sometimes confused him so much that he stopped speaking in the middle of a sentence and looked at her. This did not go unnoticed by Thea's father and brother, and they nodded their approval. In the two weeks she had spent in the house, her relatives seemed to forget about her betrayal. At the beginning of the third week, she was allowed to go out and drink coffee with her neighbours on the bench in the street. It was already mid-April and the sun had begun to warm the earth. The few tulips she had planted last year had sprouted but not yet bloomed.

Thea was seated at the left end of the bench, and two of the women who had come to drink coffee with her sat at the right-hand end, leaving a distance between her. It was a sign that they still hadn't forgiven her. One of the women was nursing her son, and Thea swallowed hard when she saw the child suckling. It all reminded her of her daughter, and she tried to look away but couldn't. She was watching, and without even realizing it, tears had fallen from her eyes. The look her older neighbour gave her startled Thea. She wiped her tears and looked at the cup of coffee she was holding in her hands. Thea had let her feelings get the best of her, and it didn't go unnoticed. By evening everyone in the hamlet would be talking about it. After drinking her coffee, Thea parted ways with the two women and walked towards the old well. She was just passing the first house in the hamlet when her brother called her to turn back.

'I want to walk a little,' she explained.

'You can't go anywhere. Go back to the house.'

Thea protested no more; she turned and walked back. As she approached the third house, she heard a car driving down the road. She turned to see it was the courier's van. A man in his thirties stopped the vehicle and got out, looking straight at her. Thea paused for a moment and blinked twice, realizing that this was her connection to the outside world. She wanted to go back and talk to the courier, but her brother had already approached her and taking her by the elbow, told her to go home. Thea lowered her head and continued towards the house. She hoped the courier had recognized her and would tell Koev that she was alive. A small smile appeared on her face. The appearance of this man gave her the strength to continue what she had started.

A few hours later, Koev was talking to his colleague Savov.

'Are you sure you saw her? Is she okay?'

'Thea looked fine. She stopped in the road as if to make sure I had seen her.'

'Was she limping? Were there facial wounds?'

'I didn't get to look at her much because her brother approached her and made her go back into the house, but she entered the sixth house, her father's home.'

'Great,' said Koev. He knew she was alive. Previously, two women from the hamlet had talked about her in front of the courier, discussing how the family had spared her life, but Savov had not seen her with his own eyes until now. Koev had been worried all the time whether he had made a mistake in bringing her back there. But now he felt he had made the right decision. If they allowed Thea to go out on the street, then she had managed to convince them of the story they made up. Now she had to find a way to tell him what she had learned, and Koev couldn't wait to hear her voice. Was she still scared? Had she refused to cooperate with them? A thousand questions were running through his head. He had to be patient and wait at least a few more days to find out what Thea would say.

Koev looked out the window and thought that all those people who were going to work and swearing at the traffic hardly knew that people like her existed. Even if he told someone that just a few miles away someone was selling their child, they would hardly believe him. That was the bane of his work. He could not share with anyone but his colleagues what was bothering him. No one else would understand. His profession limited his social life, and with each passing year, Koev felt more and more lonely. Recently he had even considered getting a cat or a dog, someone to wait for him on days like these. However, the long hours he worked quickly dissuaded him from this idea. He didn't want to leave the animal alone at home for long, and pets were not allowed at work.

It reminded him of one of the small provincial police departments where he had worked briefly. To his surprise, all the policemen brought their children and pets to work. Two women looked after them while their parents were busy. At first, Koev had been against this; he thought that the proximity of children and pets would distract the policemen and inspectors from their work, but after two weeks he agreed that, on the contrary, it made them calmer, and they were in no hurry to go home. Koev had admitted that the idea was very good. However, his superiors in Sofia did not agree with this.

He knew that in this case, it was different, and they were right. Physical evidence, murder and rape cases were not something to have near children. *Or pets,* Koev thought, and his thoughts drifted back to Thea again. She had taken a great risk to escape the hamlet. Koev secretly admired her courage and her willingness to do everything possible to find her child. However, the chances of finding Maria were diminishing with each passing day. The probability that the baby was already out of the country was high, but Koev did not want to share this with her. His conscience was guilty because he had sent her back to the hamlet, and his act was selfish. He wanted to find all the children, every last one, and entrust them to people who deserved to take care of them.

At the beginning of his career, Koev worked harder than everyone else. He almost never went out for a beer with friends because he didn't have any. One of his colleagues, trying to fit him into the team, finally asked him what his problem was. Koev then admitted to him, 'I can't stop when I know there are abandoned children on the street. If I know their names, it gets even worse.'

'But why do you take everything so personally?'

'Because I was one of them,' Koev had answered, and his colleague did not invite him to drink beer anymore. People didn't know how to deal with grown children abandoned and betrayed by their families, so they simply stopped talking to them. That was the easiest way, otherwise they had to think about every word they said so as not to hurt their feelings. And in fact, they were the ones who were hurt. The lack of a similar experience made them weak and unable to communicate. Koev had given up on explaining to everyone that he was a man like any other, only raised differently by the wrong people. Instead, he had withdrawn into himself from an early age and for years devoted all his time and attention to his work. Until he felt lonely. Then, he would go home and indulge in his depression, which he preferred no one know about.

6

Thea was cooking in the kitchen when she heard the front door open. At first, she thought it was her mother, but then she turned and saw her cousin Benny. The young woman was four months pregnant, and her belly was already protruding slightly.

'Hi. Would you like a cup of tea?' Thea asked her.

'Yes. Can I sit here with you for a while?'

'Of course.'

Thea turned on the kettle and after the water was warm, she made some tea and left it in front of Benny.

'How do you feel?'

'Not very well. I keep vomiting in the morning. My legs have started swelling too.'

'Have you tried a cold compress? Maybe it's good to make a compress with cold water.'

'Maybe I will,' Benny said quietly, and it became clear to Thea that her cousin hadn't come to her just to complain about her pregnancy. She looked at her and saw the fear in her eyes. However, Thea decided not to ask questions, but to let Benny tell her why she had come. The pregnant woman sat, swirling the teacup for a while, then dropped her hands in her lap.

'They won't let me keep it, will they?' she whispered softly.

'I don't know, Benny.'

'I heard them talking yesterday,' the pregnant woman said quietly.

'Talk about what?'

'About my baby. They want me to give birth like you here, and new parents to come and get it.'

Thea didn't answer. She didn't want to show her excitement because it might turn out that Georgi had sent Benny to talk to her.

'I can't imagine that they will take my baby away.'

'They might not.'

'The baby is not Boyan's. He doesn't want it. He doesn't even want to hear that we will keep it. He has started calling the baby a bastard. They're going to take it from me, Thea. They will take my baby away like they took your daughter.'

The mention of her daughter startled Thea. She tried to take a deep breath and stop the tears she felt coming, but she couldn't. Feelings overwhelmed her, and she sat down in the chair, hugging her cousin and sobbing. Benny was crying too.

'Now I understand what happened to you,' said the pregnant woman. 'Let's run away, Thea. Let's go to the police. I'll tell them that you said the truth and they really took your baby.'

'They won't believe us, Benny. No one will believe the story of two women from the hamlet.'

'There has to be way to do something and stop them.' Benny was crying.

'We'll figure something out. But for now, you better calm down. If my dad catches us talking about this, he'll lock us both up for a long time.'

Benny wiped her eyes and reached for the still-warm cup of tea again. 'Can you help me?'

'I don't know how I could help you, but you can come here whenever you feel like it.'

'Okay. I will say that I come to learn to cook from you. Boyan keeps telling me that I'm a bad cook.'

'All the men here say so, but in the end of the day they eat whatever you put on their plate.'

Benny smiled slightly and took a sip of her tea. 'What will you do now? The rumour on the street is that your father has found you a fiancé. Some cousin of your sister's husband.'

'What?' Thea asked. The news that her father wanted to marry her off and send her away terrified her. It hadn't occurred to her that they might want to move her.

'Rado told Boyan that as soon as your bruises are gone and you recover from the pregnancy, you will be married to someone from the village where your sister moved. They don't want to let you live here because some people in the hamlet think it's not fair to spare you. It makes trouble, you know.'

'I know,' Thea whispered. Everything was going wrong. Her long-term plan had changed. She had to do something to postpone her relocation by a few months. At least until Benny gave birth, or until she got the information she needed from Georgi.

'Are you okay?' Benny asked her, noticing Thea's paleness.

'Yes, I was just surprised that someone agreed to marry me.'

'What doesn't money do?'

'What? Did they pay someone to marry me?'

Benny nodded, and Thea could see on her face that she was already sorry for talking about it. She got up from her chair, said goodbye to Thea, and left.

Left alone in the kitchen, Thea sat on a chair and tried to make sense of what she had heard. Her family wanted to send her away so that her presence would not cause problems. Actually, the people on the street were right; her father had spared her because she was his daughter. If Benny had done what Thea had done and returned to the hamlet, the men would have met her with stones and rods. She probably would have lived, for there had been no death after these beatings for twenty years, but she certainly would not be able to move well, and her face would be disfigured for much longer. Thea had been treated more lightly, and it would not be forgotten for a long time by all their neighbours, even those who were on her side.

Thea's father had made the only right decision. He had to move her, but since she was disgraced, no one would agree to marry her for free. The tradition was that the man paid a good price for the bride to the parents, and the more beautiful the girl, the more money she was worth. In Thea's case, however, her family had to pay someone just to take her away.

Who was her fiancé, Thea wondered. She had to learn who he was and find a way to contact Koev and tell him that their plans to seduce Georgi had failed. Thea was already convinced that Georgi was coming to make sure with his own eyes that she really regretted her escape. Even if he had a crush on her, he wouldn't let his reputation be tarnished with a woman like her. She was already spoiled. Thea had to do something to change things, and she had to act fast. Once she was taken away from here, the chance of her finding out what happened to her child was nil.

A few hours later, Thea and her mother sat on the bench in front of the house. For years, Thea's mother only talked to her about household matters. The two never shared anything too personal and often learned what the other was up to from neighbourhood gossip. This time, however, Thea had decided to ask questions. She pressed her palms together nervously, wondering how to begin.

'I found out that my father has found me a fiancé,' she said and looked at her mother's face.

'Who told you?'

'Benny mentioned it today while I was showing her how to cook.'

Thea's mother said nothing. She had stared at one of the children playing in the street.

'Is it true?'

'It is true. You should be grateful that Petar agreed to marry you.'

Thea knew Petar, and the mere mention of his name made her skin crawl. The Baron, as everyone called him, had a bad reputation. He had been to prison several times already, once narrowly escaping conviction for the attempted murder of his ex-girlfriend.

'He is bad man. He will beat me,' Thea said quietly. Her mother turned and glared at her. 'What did you expect? Stay here and keep causing trouble?'

'No, but ...'

'The Baron is the only one who agreed to take you.'

'I don't want to marry him.'

'You have no choice. In two weeks, preparations for the wedding will be ready. Until then, my advice is to put your head down and put up with it. You have only yourself to blame for the fate that awaits you.'

Thea was surprised by the tone in which her mother spoke to her.

'Okay, I'll go live with him. But let me ask you something. What have I done to you to be so rude to me? You've been doing it for many years.'

Kina stared at the road for a moment, then turned to Thea and looked into her eyes. 'What I wouldn't give to have your beauty and your mind, Thea. Until recently, I, envied you. Yes, I, your own mother, envied you. I thought you would get out of here, that you would accept your teacher's help and go study. Do you know she came here twice to talk to me?'

'No. I did not.'

'Mrs. Mariola wanted to take you to her place. She even wanted to pay us, but I wouldn't agree. I wanted to see how you would gather your strength and escape from this hell on your own. Instead, you went off the deep end.'

Thea was shocked by what her mother said. Envy, that's what had driven them apart.

'You could have told me.'

'And admit that I envy my youngest daughter? I would never do that.'

'But now you're telling me,' Thea whispered.

'I told you because I know that once you leave here, I won't see you again.'

Thea's eyes widened in horror. Her father had not paid Petar to marry her, but to kill her. Her family and Georgi did not believe her story. They had let her live because they knew the police would be looking for her. However, if she married The Baron, she was no longer their responsibility, but his. Perhaps her husband-to-be was even now planning exactly how to kill her.

Thea couldn't sleep all night. If what her mother said was true, then she only had two weeks to turn things around. She had to find a way to convince Georgi and her family not to send her away.

Thea sat down on the old sofa in the kitchen, where she had slept since she was a child. She had to make a plan that would work quickly. However, just in case, she decided to prepare for the worst situation, so she got up, took a small knife, and put it under her pillow. She had to find a way to protect herself if things got rough.

Thea stared out the window and began mentally adding and discarding options to help her get out of the situation. One option was to repay her debt to her family and to the hamlet. If she could find the money that they had paid The Baron, she might be able to get away. Thea had to make sure that the people here needed her. Then chance of her being sent away was less. For these people, honour came second to money. If she found a way to give them money regularly, no one would vote to kick her out. Maybe Koev would help her with that, she thought, and that thought somehow calmed her down. Thea wrapped herself in the old blanket and decided that the morning would surely be smarter than the evening. Then she relaxed and fell asleep after a few minutes.

In the morning, Benny visited her again. Thea asked her to take a walk and led her to the old well. Her cousin did not stop talking; she was scared and worried about her unborn baby. Thea listened, and when they reached the well, she leaned against the stone, which was marked with rust. She kept the conversation going with Benny and at the same time tried to get out what was left under the stone. To her surprise, her hands found only paper. Koev had left her a note.

'What is in this well now?' Thea asked, pulling the note out from under the stone and quickly reading it while looking down. The note said that the camera had sound and Thea just had to talk. She breathed a sigh of relief and turned back to Benny. Her cousin was sitting across from her on an old tree stump, rubbing her ankles.

'I remember how my legs hurt when I was pregnant,' said Thea sympathetically.

'I try to put on cold compresses, but Boyan won't let me. He wants me to be around him all the time while he's at home and to pay attention to him only.'

'How did he accept the affair?'

'Not good. He still wants to go and kill him. Every time he came to the hamlet ...'

Benny stopped talking as if she had said something she didn't want to share.

'Who came to the hamlet? The father of your baby? Who is he?'

Benny turned to face the road. Thea could tell she didn't want to talk about it, but she wouldn't let her. She insisted on finding out who the baby's father was, and the moment she heard his name, at first Thea was surprised, then decided that Georgi had managed to seduce another fool.

'Who else knows?'

'Only me and Boyan. Now you know too, but please don't tell anyone else.'

'Everyone knows that Boyan is not the father. Who did you tell my dad the man you cheated with was?'

'We told him that I went to the city and met someone there. A tourist.'

'A tourist? And he believed you?'

'Boyan said he saw us.'

'Benny, you must tell my father the truth. Georgi uses the women in the hamlet.'

'Are you jealous?' Benny asked.

'To be honest, no.'

'Okay. Because I keep on ... you get the idea.'

Thea opened her mouth in surprise and was about to say something but couldn't. What her cousin said confused her. Maybe Georgi was using Benny to find out what Thea was up to after all.

'I'm not jealous, but I admit that I still have feelings for him,' she said. 'I don't want to move, and I don't want to get married because I still love him. Petar... The Baron... won't be able to replace him. That's why I don't want to marry him.'

Thea continued to lean against the well and hoped that Koev or one of his team could hear the conversation.

'And if I were you, I wouldn't want to have anything to do with The Baron. He's a dangerous man, Thea. You must beware of him.'

'I know. I hope my father will change his mind and not send me away.'

'I don't think so. Yesterday, my neighbour told me that at the end of the month, The Baron is getting out of prison and will come to pick you up right away.'

Thea shivered unconsciously. Just the thought that this man would have the right to touch her made her go crazy.

'How much money did they pay him?' she wondered.

'As far as I know, your father offered five thousand to anyone who wanted to take you as his wife.'

'Is my life worth that much?'

'Your life is worth nothing, Thea. You're the smart one in the hamlet; you should have figured that out by now.'

Benny got up slowly and headed for the road. Thea followed her with her eyes, and when she judged that her cousin was far enough away not to hear her, she turned to face the well.

'Help me! Make sure The Baron doesn't take me out of the hamlet. They paid him five thousand euro. If I return the money and somehow bring income to the people here, they might leave me alone.'

Thea heard a noise behind her and immediately started humming. When she turned around, she saw Georgi walking towards her.

'Are you talking to yourself?' he asked her.

'No, I'm singing,' she said and continued to sing one of the love songs she loved as a child.

'Strange,' he said. 'I thought you were talking to yourself.'

'No. I remembered some things.' She gently smiled. 'Something about you.'

'About me? And what is it?'

Thea moved closer to him, lifted her head, and looked into his eyes.

'Do you remember when we got lonely once not far from here?'

'Aha.'

Georgi looked at her, then abruptly grabbed her hands and forced her to turn her back to him.

'What are you hiding?' he asked and began to search her.

'Nothing,' she cried, trying to free herself.

'You're hiding something. Do you have a phone?'

'I swear, I have nothing.'

'I'm sure you were talking to someone,' he said through his teeth and roughly turned her towards him. 'Strip! Immediately!'

Thea cried and began to slowly remove her clothes. What was happening attracted the attention of the people of the hamlet. Everyone sat to the side and watched as Thea took off first her sweater, then the T-shirt underneath. Georgi gestured for her to take off her bra as well. She handed him her clothes, and he carefully examined each item. Georgi did the same with her jeans and shoes, and when Thea was left in just her panties, he moved closer to her and groped her thoroughly, leaving his hands on her body for longer than necessary. Finding nothing, Georgi looked into her eyes. His gaze was urgent, as if he wanted her to confess something. However, Thea lowered her eyes and tried to cover her breasts with her hands.

'You really were humming.' He smiled at her, but his eyes did not register the feeling. 'You can get dressed now.'

She quickly put on her shoes and jeans, then threw on her sweater and headed to her family's house. As she walked, Thea continued to cry from the humiliation she had experienced. The crowd of onlookers made way for her to pass, and they all slowly followed her down the road. When she entered the house, Thea sat down on the sofa close to her mother, and her body began to tremble. She had never been so afraid or humiliated in her life. What happened at the old well shook her deeply. And not only her. Koev, who was watching what was happening on his phone, was also shocked by the way Georgi and the people of the hamlet treated her.

As luck would have it, Thea had thrown the note into the well and hadn't kept it. If Georgi had found it, she would not have gotten out of there alive; Koev was convinced of that. Things had gotten out of hand, and he and his team had to find a way to help her regain the village's trust in her. Koev already knew what he was going to do about The Baron. He was going to make sure that he stayed in prison for a few more months. But about the money Thea had to pay for her freedom, Koev had no idea how they could do that without anyone suspecting her. They needed time, and they didn't have it. Koev sighed and rewound the tape to where Thea was begging him for help. She looked so helpless that his heart sank as he looked at her.

7

Two days had passed since Georgi had found her at the old well. In those two days he visited her twice. Each time he stood in front of her and looked her straight in the eyes, waiting for her to say something, but she didn't speak. Thea could feel that she had challenged him with something, and he was nervous. Thea didn't know what to say or do, so she kept quiet, and her silence was obviously driving him crazy. Every time Georgi entered the house, there was tension between the two of them. Her father and brother were annoyed by this and gave her displeased looks. At the end of the second day, her mother came home and told her that The Baron had an extended sentence for a few more months and wouldn't be coming to pick her up anytime soon. Koev had heard what she said, Thea thought, and sighed with relief. One of her problems was solved, but she had to deal with the money problem quickly.

One day, while cooking in the kitchen, Thea heard an argument on the road and went out to see what was going on. Three social workers were outside with laptops and folders, and they were arguing with one of the families.

'You have not sent us the necessary documents,' explained the woman. 'Until you send them, you will not receive benefits.'

'Then let us sign them now,' pleaded the mother of the three children who were standing next to her.

'You have to send them online, as I already told you. Now everything is done through email.'

'We don't have that.'

Thea approached them.

'I have an email. We can send the documents through mine, right?'

The social worker nodded.

'Don't worry, I'll help you.' Thea turned to the family. 'What documents do we need?'

'Here is the list. If you don't send everything by tomorrow morning, I will have to stop the benefits.'

'We will send them, I promise.'

'Okay then,' said the woman and motioned for her colleagues to leave.

Thea looked at them and thought that this was a good opportunity to be useful to the hamlet. She looked at the list of documents they needed and turned to her neighbour.

'Bring me the documents and ask Rado to lend us his phone and laptop.'

'Are you sure you can handle this ...'

'Email? Yes, I can do it. Just bring me what I asked you for.'

'Okay.'

Two hours later, Thea successfully submitted the required documents and, in the morning, received confirmation that the benefits would not be suspended. From that day until the end of the week, almost all of the hamlet families visited her, asking her to help them with one thing or another that needed to be done on the internet. During this time, everyone seemed to forget about her betrayal and started inviting her to their celebrations, some even paying her for the services she did for them. One of these celebrations was in the first house that was near the old well. Thea played with one of the children and deliberately threw his ball into the well. When she came over to pick it up, she laughed at the child, then quickly turned to the camera, and said that she had managed to find a way to win people over here.

Koev, who subsequently watches the recording, smiled. Thea was a resourceful and strong woman, and she hadn't even realized it. A team of five people were working on a project to get her the money she needed, and now she had found a solution to this problem herself. At that moment, Koev realized that she would do it; she would find a way to wrap Georgi around her little finger again and find her daughter. The other thought that immediately came to mind was that she didn't need the Regional Police Department; they needed her.

***

Thea worked a lot, but someone was always standing by her side. Her family and Georgi wouldn't let her use the phone or the internet without one of them being there. Then her brother would check who she was emailing. He was careful, and even though she was now being given more freedom, Thea realized that she was still being treated like a prisoner. Outside the family, no one seemed to suspect that her relatives did not trust her, but inside the house, Thea could feel the scrutiny. Georgi came more and more often, and this time he only drank beer with her brother or her father and talked with them but did not pay her any attention.

One night he stayed late, had dinner at their house and asked her family to leave him alone with her. Thea was surprised and tried not to show her concern. She was sitting on the sofa in the kitchen reading a book when she felt him sit down next to her.

'You're a big mystery to me, Thea,' he said and took the book she was holding, put it aside, and took one of her hands. He started caressing the inside of her palm and looked for her reaction. Thea hadn't expected him to be gentle with her. She thought Georgi would attack her roughly or try to kiss her, but he did nothing of the sort. Instead, he continued to caress her hand and watch her.

'You like it, don't you?' he asked her.

'Yes,' Thea said and admitted to herself that she wasn't lying. She really liked his touch. She looked at him, and he was smiling at her.

'I thought you were trying to seduce me at the old well and hide something from me, but now I understand that I was wrong,' he whispered and leaned towards her and kissed her gently behind the ear. Thea gasped at his touch.

'We can have a good time together, you know?' he said.

She didn't answer. She let him kiss her neck. Then she pushed him away.

'I'm hardly of any interest to you anymore. I can't give you anything you haven't already had.'

Georgi tried to kiss her again, but she pushed him away again.

'I will tarnish your reputation,' she said and stroked his arm gently, the way he had done with her. Georgi's pupils widened.

'Thea, there is no one like you. For months I tried to forget you, to tell myself that I shouldn't trust you, but you are the devil, and you got under my skin.'

'But you agreed I could marry someone else,' she reproached him, trying to keep the gentle note in her voice. 'You quickly gave up on me.'

'He won't be getting out of prison anytime soon.'

'And after he leaves, he will take me with him.'

'Let's not talk about it now.'

'Okay,' she agreed and got up from the sofa. He followed her with his eyes, then got up and left the house. Thea smiled. Mary was right, Georgi was infatuated with her, and she was going to use him the way he had used her. She would betray him. Before that, though, she had to do her best to get close to him.

***

A month later, Thea was free to go anywhere. No one restricted her from going out or using the laptop and phone her family had bought to support her new 'business'. Georgi visited her often in the hope that she would forgive him and sleep with him again, but she gently pushed him away each time. His infatuation with her was so obvious that it was rumoured in the hamlet that he had left his wife for Thea. Whether that was true or not, Thea had no way of knowing, for although she could walk freely in the hamlet, she had not yet left it. She had contacted Koev on the internet, and the two were now exchanging secret e-mails. However, both sides had nothing new to share. All Thea wanted to know was if they had found any information about her daughter, but unfortunately, there was no new information. Maria had been taken somewhere, and Thea was going crazy worrying that something bad had happened to her. Of course, she didn't share her concerns with anyone in the hamlet. Only Benny felt her pain. The two women became very close. Thea's cousin's baby was due in August, and with each passing day, Benny grew more anxious and cried more often.

'You need to calm down. Stress is not good for you or your baby.'

'But what can I do, Thea? They will take my child.'

'They might not take it away.'

'They will sell it. Yesterday Boyan confirmed the price. They will pay 60,000 euros if it's a boy and 50,000 if it's a girl.'

It was the first time Thea had heard anything concrete. Her heart began to beat faster.

'Who told you?'

'Boyan.'

'He probably shares everything with you, huh?'

'Yes, when he gets drunk, he tells me everything. That's why I'm sure they'll take my child away.'

'Why don't you talk to Georgi?'

'He doesn't want the baby. All that devil wants right now is you and money. He is not interested in anything else. Only you can make him stop the deal. Please, Thea, talk to him. He will do anything for you.'

'He sold our baby, Benny. I don't think I can talk to him about it. You should talk to him. After all, you are the mother, and he is the father.'

Benny cried again, and Thea felt sorry for her. The young woman looked desperate and helpless. Thea secretly hoped she could help her and stop the deal before they took her baby, but it all depended on how much Georgi would believe her that she was still in love with him. The game Thea was playing was a dangerous one, and she knew it. Georgi could quickly lose interest in her, and that was what worried her the most.

For several days, Georgi came every evening to her father's house. He often sat in a chair and watched Thea work on the laptop. The need for her services grew more and more, and soon the mere mention of her leaving the hamlet caused people to become displeased. As she herself had said, with these people, money was more important than honour. Thea could feel Georgi's testing gaze and wondered how this would all end. One evening, her mother and father left her alone with him. Thea was sitting on the small kitchen sofa, and Georgi had settled on a chair near her. Realizing that they were alone, she reached for one of the books she was reading, but Georgi got up and took her hand. Then he sat down next to her.

'You know why we are alone, Thea.'

She looked at him and pushed his hand away and got up from the sofa.

'I know, and I think this will be a mistake. I understand you have a wife and children. I didn't know about them before, but now that I do, I can't give you what you want.'

'Why not?'

Georgi also got up and approached her, trying to hug her and pull her to him. Thea crossed her arms over her chest and moved again, this time heading for the living room.

'You know you can't refuse me. You belong to me.'

'But you quickly gave me to another man.'

'That was a mistake. You don't have to worry about Petar anymore. I paid him the money and he won't come looking for you.'

Thea breathed a sigh of relief. She was more afraid of The Baron than of Georgi.

'Can you see now what I'm doing for you, Thea? I have never paid so much for a woman before.'

'Is that what you measure women by? Money? How much you will you spend on a woman determines her worth? Well, let me tell you, I'm not that cheap. If you want to have me again, you will have to try harder. I want to have everything your wife has. I want to go to restaurants and sleep at your house.'

'Thea.' Georgi tried to protest, but she stopped him.

'You said you wanted me back. That's the price you'll have to pay. I want my freedom.'

'You want more than I can give you. I can't take you to my house; my wife's children are there. And you told me that you still love me; why don't we enjoy our love?'

'I love you, but I'm not a little girl anymore, and I want more. I want your respect. I want to spend more time with you, to always be by your side, do you understand?'

'I am here now.'

'That's right, but you'll be leaving in an hour. And then what? Are you going to leave me again?'

'I will not leave you and I will prove it.'

'Okay. Prove it.'

Georgi, feeling that he was losing the argument, approached Thea, and tried to draw her to him again. She didn't pull away, let him kiss her. Then she looked into his eyes and opened the front door for him, gesturing to leave the house.

'Are you sending me away?'

'Yes.'

'No one has done it before,' he said and smiled. He walked slowly to the entrance and stared at her. 'I will be back soon.'

'I will wait for you,' Thea told him, and to his surprise she approached him and kissed him. This seemed to confuse him even more. Georgi walked up the road, then realized that he had gone in the wrong direction, and he turned back, waved goodbye to her, and continued the right way. Several people were sitting on the benches in front of their houses, watching the scene. Never before had anyone shown feelings and intimacy on the street like this. Whatever happened, happened inside the houses, and no one talked about it. The fact that Georgi had allowed himself to be kissed in public stirred up the hamlet. It was already clear to everyone that he was madly in love and that Thea had him wrapped around her little finger.

After saying goodbye to Georgi, Thea wrote an email to Koev, in which she informed him that The Baron was no longer a threat to her, and that Georgi had paid her debt to him. Thea knew she had taken a risky approach, but she didn't regret it. She would do anything for Georgi to invite her to his home. Her conscience was gnawing at her for Georgi's wife and children. She didn't want to hurt them in any way, but she had no choice. And according to rumours, his wife had not lived with him for a long time. Georgi was the only person who knew where her daughter was, and Thea would do anything to find her.

When her father and brother returned to the house, they called her into the living room. They didn't look pleased.

'What game are you playing?' Rado asked her.

'None.'

'I know you well. You can lie to anyone else, but not me.' He raised his voice and pounded his fist on the table.

'Georgi wants to spend an hour or two with me, and I want more. Is it bad to want to be with him longer?'

'I don't believe you.' Her father also frowned. 'You are planning something in that beautiful head of yours. You better tell me what you're up to.'

'I haven't thought of anything. I told him that I was worth more and that if he really loved me, he would have to show me that I was more than a one-night stand, live with me, go out with me, and give me my freedom back.'

'You are free now. Georgi has paid off your debt to The Baron,' said Rado and continued to watch her testily.

'That's what he told me, but that doesn't mean he won't change his mind tomorrow. I need to be sure of a good life in the meantime.'

'You know that if he starts giving you money, half of it belongs to us, right?' her father said, and only now did Thea understand what the purpose of this conversation was. They wanted the money; they didn't care how she was or what would happen to her. Her family wanted to make sure that they would be part of the game.

'Half of all my money will be yours.'

'Good, good,' her father said and lay down on the sofa.

'Still, be careful with Georgi, Thea. He is crazy and unpredictable,' warned Rado and she saw concern in his eyes. Her brother was worried about her, she realized. Thea walked past him and gave him a friendly pat on the shoulder. 'Don't worry about me. Everything will be fine.'

Thea walked into the kitchen, and shortly after, her mother joined her.

'You don't give up easily,' Kina said. 'I expected you to do something, but you're being braver than I've ever been.'

Thea looked at her mother and saw for the first time the wrinkles around her mouth and eyes. Kina had aged in just a year. Obviously, what was happening with her family was bothering her, and Thea blamed herself for not noticing that. She had been caught up in her own problems and hadn't considered that her mother was also suffering. The two of them never talked about the baby, never mentioned the day Maria was born. What had made her mother willingly give the child to other people? Thea decided that she should ask her someday, but today just wasn't the time. Now she had to focus on the present and find a way to get the information she needed.

To Thea's surprise, Georgi did not show up for the next two days. Waiting for him to come made her nervous. She listened to every noise in the hamlet. She went outside the house every time she heard a car approaching. It reminded her of the times when she was truly in love with Georgi. The anticipation and trepidation that she would see him. But now Thea's feelings were different. She was filled with fear and doubt. What if Georgi came to his senses and didn't come back? What if he found out she was working with the police? What if ...? Thousands of questions were running through her head, so when she saw him walk through the front door with a big smile on his face, she was really happy to see him. Georgi accepted her smile as a warm welcome, picked her up with his hands, and kissed her.

'Come on, princess, I'll take you to dinner.'

'Where?'

'Surprise.'

'What should I wear?' she asked and showed him with a gesture the clothes she was wearing.

'I brought you clothes. They are in the trunk of the car.'

Georgi took her by the hand and led her to the car to show her the clothes he had bought for her. At that moment, Thea realized that he really was madly in love. It wasn't a pretence. Georgi was smiling, holding her hand, and looking at her with a twinkle in his eyes. It was so unexpected that she stood looking at him in amazement and didn't know how to react. Her confusion was obvious, but Georgi didn't seem to notice it. He took the expensive clothes and jewellery he had bought her out of the bags and showed her the purchases with a big smile on his face.

'You can wear the red dress. Red suits you very well.'

'Okay.'

'After dinner we will go home.'

'What about your wife and children?' she asked.

'They are at the mother-in-law's house. It's just you and me tonight.'

Thea swallowed hard. She didn't expect events to unfold so quickly. After changing and fixing her hair, Thea let Georgi walk her to the car. He opened the door to help her settle into the seat in the long red dress. He was right, the dress suited her.

The restaurant they dined at was nice, but Thea didn't get to enjoy the food. Just the thought of having to spend the night with Georgi made her stomach churn. On top of that, while they were eating, Mrs. Mariola passed by them, and the shock of seeing her in the company of Georgi was written on her face. Then Thea saw the disappointment in the teacher's eyes. The old woman passed, and her body seemed to hunch over. *What had she been thinking?* Thea wondered.

'Do you like it here?' asked Georgi, who had also seen Mrs. Mariola.

'Yes. It is very pleasant, and the food is delicious.'

'You can order something else. If you want to eat something special, Pepi will make it for you. He is a good cook, but running a restaurant is not his thing. He needed help.'

'And you helped him.'

'Yes. I have a good heart – I help anyone in need. I have helped most people in this town.'

'I didn't know that.'

'There are many things you don't know about me, Thea, but we will soon change that. Do you know what I was thinking the other day after I got home from the hamlet?'

'No. What were you thinking?'

'I thought you and I are a wonderful couple. We are both smart and beautiful. We both had hard childhoods and parents who are willing to sell us for a few grand.'

'I didn't know about your parents. Where do they live?'

'North.'

'When was the last time you saw them?'

'Twenty years ago,' said Georgi, and from the sound of his voice, Thea could feel his sadness. His memories probably weren't good. The man standing before her now was different from the one she had known before. Georgi had always been aware of what he was doing, with the self-confidence that he was unattainable and that he had power over everything. But now he was vulnerable, and he talked to her about things that were bothering him. He told her about his childhood and the time when, after he tried to run away from home at the age of sixteen, his father beat him badly and locked him in the house for a long time.

'Two years later I ran away and never returned there. And now every time I visit your father's house, I feel like you want to run away from there too. Am I right?'

His question surprised Thea. She wondered again if he was playing a role.

'Yes, sometimes I want to get out of there.'

'Good.' He smiled and fixed her with a bright look.

What is he up to? she wondered. They stayed in the restaurant for another hour. Then Georgi took her to his house. The house wasn't big, but it was kind of empty. There was furniture, but no personal items.

'I had Ivana move out a while ago. You can change the furniture if you don't like it.'

'Do you want me to live here with you?' Thea asked in astonishment.

'Yes. This is your home now.'

'And the kids? What will happen to them?'

The mention of children made him frown. 'Their mother will take care of them. They are not my problem. And now that you've opened this topic, I want you to promise me that you won't surprise me like last time. No pregnancies and no children. Clear? You'll take your pills regularly, and you won't do anything stupid.'

The tone in which he spoke to her had changed. He had become strict and insistent. While he was talking to her, Georgi had grabbed her chin and raised her head so that he was looking directly into her eyes. Then, realizing that he was causing her pain, he lowered his hand and kissed her gently.

'No children. Are we clear?'

'Yes, I understand.'

'You can look around the house. I'll find you in a few minutes.'

Thea toured the lower floor first. The kitchen was well equipped, and the fridge and freezer were stocked with food. Then she went up to the second floor, where, apart from two bedrooms and a bathroom, there was a room where Georgi had locked himself in, and she could hear that he was talking to someone on the phone. Thea tried to figure out what the conversation was about, but she only heard fragments and gave up. She went into one of the bedrooms and opened the wardrobe. There were hardly any clothes in it.

'We will buy you everything you need,' said Georgi, appearing in the doorway.

'And where are your clothes? Won't you live here with me?'

'I just need a few things. I don't like to collect clothes and personal belongings. Come now, let's have fun.'

Georgi pulled her to him, then led her gently to the bed. Thea closed her eyes and tried to imagine that the person she was supposed to spend the night with was someone else. Thus, the betrayal she committed against herself would be more tolerable.

8

In the morning, when Thea woke up, Georgi was gone. He had left her a phone on the kitchen counter and a note to call him when she woke up. But she didn't. Instead, she hurriedly put on the jeans and T-shirt he had left her and began to walk around the house, hoping to find some information about her daughter and the other children. Thea rummaged through all the lockers and wardrobes. She turned the entire house over, hoping to find something hidden there. Everywhere was clean, as if no one had lived in this house before. The only place Thea couldn't go in and check for any information was the room where Georgi had gone in the evening. Thea went out into the garden and looked into the window of the locked room. The window was high up, and it would be difficult for Thea to climb up there without one of the neighbours seeing her. She had to find another way to get into the locked room. When she got back inside the house, Georgi was waiting for her in the kitchen.

'Good morning,' she greeted him.

'Why didn't you call me?'

'I saw the garden and decided to go and look at it. I thought it would be nice to plant roses.'

Thea turned her back on Georgi, and only knew something was wrong when she felt pain. Georgi grabbed her hair and pulled her towards the kitchen counter.

'I knew I couldn't trust you. Bitch. Don't you think I'm going to leave you alone here and do whatever you want? I saw you looking at the window. You have no interest in flowers.'

Thea screamed in pain, but he seemed to like it.

'Are you working with the police?' he shouted in her ear.

'No. I was wondering why you lock yourself in that room. Please, Georgi, let me explain.'

He continued to press her head against the counter, and when Thea met his eyes, she saw the madness in them. She had to calm him down or he would kill her; she was sure of it.

'You said that I could go into any room, but not that one. You were talking to someone inside last night. I figured you were hiding another woman, so I wanted to look inside. Please let me go.'

'You're lying.'

'I don't lie. Please, think about it. If you were me, wouldn't you think I was hiding a lover in this room?'

Georgi's grip loosened, and he seemed to calm down. He turned Thea's face towards him and kissed her. First gently, then more insistently.

'You're right, I was going to think that too. Come, I will show you the room and you will see with your own eyes that there is no one inside.'

Thea stood up slowly, still unsure of his next move. Then she followed him up the stairs. Georgi pulled out a small set of keys and unlocked the door. Then he gestured for her to come inside. The room was small. Inside was a laptop, a printer, and a desk with a chair. Thea didn't see any documents anywhere.

'You're right, I was worried about nothing,' she said.

'Are you calmer now?'

'Yes. Do you work here?'

'Sometimes. But I mostly meet my clients outside the house. Why do you ask?'

'I can make you coffee when you work here.'

'You know what, princess, I haven't had coffee in my office before. I might start spending more time at home.' He laughed and pulled her to the bed in the other bedroom.

Two hours later, Georgi took her to Sofia to buy her everything she would need for the house. While she was shopping, he was on the phone. Thea tried to figure out who he was talking to and what he was talking about, and sometimes managed to string a few sentences together. After they returned to Bolengrad, he continued to talk on the phone without worrying about her. At the end of the third day, she already knew the names or nicknames of the people with whom Georgi made deals, but most of them were related to money lent or bets. None of the conversations Thea heard were related to child trafficking. However, what she was able to establish was that Koev was right, Georgi had a second phone. Most of his conversations during the day were on his personal phone, but every night between nine and ten o'clock, he locked himself in his small office and talked on the other. Thea couldn't hear the conversations very well. She heard only fragmentary phrases and could never make out who he was talking to. She never saw the laptop that was in the room turned on, and it remained a mystery to her what Georgi was using it for.

Georgi had warned Thea not to leave the house without him. The phone he had left for her was only to call her parents and him, so she could not and did not want to use it as a connection with Koev. For the first few days, Thea wondered how to inform him that she was no longer in the hamlet, then it occurred to her to order something online and use the courier's phone. To her surprise, the person who brought her the package was the same person who visited the hamlet.

'We've been watching the house, and we know you've been here for a few days.'

'Georgi has a second phone in one of the rooms, but I can't go in there.'

'Okay, tomorrow I'll bring you something to open the door with.'

Thea quickly told him what she knew, pretending there was a problem with the shipment. Finally, she gave it back to him and told him to come with a proper parcel as soon as possible. The next day, Thea waited for him to return, but he never did. He didn't come the next one, or the day after that. Her worry that something had happened to him grew. Whatever had happened, Thea had no way of knowing. The lack of information from Koev made her nervous. She wondered how to get in touch with him without Georgi suspecting. Finally, a distraction on his part hastened events. On the morning of the second week, Thea brought him coffee in the small office. Georgi had opened his laptop and was checking his bank balances. It was the first time Thea had seen him use it. She placed the coffee carefully on the desk and looked at the glowing screen. Georgi followed her gaze. Instead of sending her away, he made her sit next to him.

'Do you see how rich we are? More money will come soon,' he boasted. However, it was not the balance that Thea was looking at, but the name of the owner of the bank account. She tried to remember as much information as possible. While she was in the room, Georgi's personal phone rang, and when he reached for it, the coffee mug fell, and the hot liquid spilled onto the floor. Georgi swore, and Thea took a cloth from the kitchen and started cleaning. To her surprise, Georgi did not wait for her to finish cleaning, but left the house almost immediately. This was the chance Thea had been waiting for. After she was convinced that he had gone somewhere in the car and that she was alone, Thea took a bag, put the laptop and phone inside, closed the room and went out into the garden. She jumped over the fence and ran down the streets as fast as she could. Her target was the police station. The police building was far away, and Thea ran as fast as she could hoping none of Georgi's people would see her. She was halfway there when the phone rang. The ringing continued for a long time and attracted the attention of passers-by, so finally forced to pick up the phone, Thea stopped and pressed the green receiver.

'In half an hour, at the Blue Café, the exchange will take place. Do not be late!' said a male voice and the conversation ended.

Thea stared at the phone wondering what to do. If she went to the police station, she wouldn't have time to go to the Blue Café. If she went to the café, there was a chance that someone would recognize her and call Georgi. Thea hesitated for a while then decided it was better to go to the café and see what would happen there.

The Blue Café was one of the most popular establishments in town and was run by a middle-aged blonde. Every other person was meeting there, and it would be difficult for Thea to know who was there to meet whom, but she decided to take a chance anyway. When she arrived at the café, she went inside so there was less chance of anyone seeing her. She didn't order anything because she had no money. Thea told the waiter that she was expecting someone and looked out the window at the tables in the garden. There were no customers inside the café itself, but there were almost no seats outside. Exactly half an hour later, a man entered, went to the bar, and ordered still water. While sipping the water, the man talked to the bartender and asked him about Georgi. Thea recognized the voice on the phone and listened to what else he was going to say, but as soon as he realized that Georgi had not yet arrived, the man sat down at the next table and stared at the door of the café. A few minutes later, a young man stepped inside and began to nervously look around.

'Are you the Hat?' asked the newcomer.

'Yes. And who are you?'

'I am the exchange. Where is Georgi?'

'I don't know. I called him half an hour ago, but he hasn't come yet.'

'We will wait another five minutes. If he does not come by, then the exchange is postponed.'

'Georgi will come. He always comes on time.'

'Well, he's getting late now. Call him and tell him he only has five minutes.'

Thea cringed as she saw the man dial the number on the phone she was still holding in her hand. She reacted as quickly as possible and turn the sound off.

'Voicemail is on,' said the man and got up. 'The exchange failed. I will call for a new day and time.'

The two men left the café, and each went in a different direction, leaving Thea to wonder what had just happened. A few minutes later, she also left, and this time, without running, she headed for the police station. The moment Mirov saw her, he escorted her to one of the vacant rooms there.

'We need to contact Koev immediately,' she told him.

Mirov called someone on the phone and left Thea in a small room.

'Yes, she's with me. Okay, I'll hold her as long as I can.'

To her surprise, Mirov returned and locked the door to the room. Thea realized too late that the phone call was not to Koev. Mirov had called Georgi, and Thea realized that she had fallen into a trap. Somehow, Georgi had gotten the policeman into his game. He had found his weak spot and taken advantage of it, Thea thought, panicking. If Georgi took her from the police station, she wouldn't stay alive for long. *How long would it take him to come?* she wondered. Maybe half an hour to an hour, depending on what part of town he was in. There was still time to get out, she thought, and put the phone back together. Then she opened the laptop as well, hoping that Georgi had not set a password, but both devices were protected.

'Damn it,' she said and looked at the glowing phone. Several messages appeared on the display. She tried to open one of them and to her surprise she succeeded. It was an email sent by one of the mobile operators. Thea stared at the phone screen, then dialled the lieutenant's phone. However, no one answered on the other side of the line. Where was Koev, and why was he not picking up his phone? Then she remembered that Koev had no way of knowing that she was calling. He was unlikely to answer. Thea opened the mail and emailed the lieutenant. Now it all depended on how quickly he would read the email. He could read it right away or he could read it when it was already too late, so Thea started to write a new email with all the information she knew about Georgi, about his past, about the people he was in contact with, and about the bank accounts she had seen. As soon as she sent the email, she felt at ease. Now she only had to wait to see who would appear first – Koev or Georgi.

She stood in front of the small table, put her hands in front of her, and began to pray Koev would send help quickly. She thought about her life and how many chances she had before she met Georgi. Now at this point, Thea was convinced that if she fell into his hands again, he would kill her. One day he had told her how he had twisted the neck of one of his girlfriends. The only murder he had committed with his own hands.

'I put her head on the table, pressed her hard, and then just turned it like a steering wheel when you want to park the car in reverse. It's so easy to wring a woman's neck. Delicate, thin necks give up quickly. Remember that, Thea.'

Thea was already imagining Georgi pressing her against the table and wringing her neck when the door to the room opened and policeman Popov entered.

'Come, we have not much time,' he said and invited her to leave the room. 'Koev just called and told me to take you to Sofia as quickly as possible. Is this true about Mirov?'

'Yes. Georgi is probably threatening him with something.'

'I can't believe it,' said Popov and opened the emergency exit. Several patrol cars were parked in front of the exit, and the policeman headed towards one of them. Then he turned on the sirens and started on the road to Sofia. Thea watched him and wondered if she should believe him, or if he too was bought or threatened by Georgi. She calmed down only after Popov called Koev to tell him that she was safe.

When they arrived at Koev's office, Thea told him what she knew, handed over Georgi's laptop and phone, and waited for them to tell her if they had found any information about her daughter. Mary put Thea in her office and occasionally came to talk to her.

'You succeeded,' she told her. 'You did everything that depended on you. We were all worried about you here. And when Savov disappeared ...'

'The courier?'

'Yes. He was supposed to bring you a fake package and talk to you.'

'But he spoke to me. I told him about Georgi's office, and he said he would be back the next day with something to help me open the door.'

'Do you remember what time that was?'

'At 1 p.m.'

'Shortly after that, he disappeared. He was seen last at 2:15 p.m.'

'Did Georgi realize that he was from the police?'

'I don't think so. He would have cut you out of his life right away.'

'That's right. But what do you think happened to your colleague?'

'We don't know yet, Thea. But if you think that something happened to him because of you, then I must assure you that it is not so. Savov worked undercover as a courier on several cases.'

'I hope you find out soon what happened to him. The unknown is an unpleasant feeling. It eats you up inside and makes you ask yourself thousands of questions.'

'I know it is, and I'm really sorry for what you had to go through. Hopefully, we'll find out where your daughter is soon. You had called her Maria, hadn't you?'

'Yes, Maria.'

Thea stayed in Mary's office most of the night. Koev and his colleagues came from time to time to talk to her. Sometimes they needed information, and sometimes they talked about trivial things. By 5 a.m., Koev forced her to go to one of the apartments on the upper floor and rest.

'Cracking the laptop password turned out to be more difficult than we thought, and it may take a long time. Go get some rest. If we learn something, I promise to come right away and tell you.'

Thea didn't want to leave the office, but finally agreed. Lying in the bed, she wondered what else she had to go through to find Maria. She had no illusions that there would be a name and address in the laptop where she could find her daughter. Living even just a few days with Georgi gave her a clear idea of what kind of person he was. And he was meticulous. A person like him wouldn't leave any information just like that. Even if they cracked the passwords soon, Thea was sure they'd have to crack at least one or two more before they got to anything. The name and bank account she had told them did not produce the result Koev and Thea had expected. It turned out to be an offshore foreign account and it would take days for them to get the necessary permission to freeze it. Georgi could have withdrawn the money by then and covered his back. From what she knew of him now, he had done it before. He had changed his name and the city he lived in before, but now Thea was sure he was going to change the country as well. People like him were always prepared and had a plan B. This was the kind of person Thea was unlucky enough to get involved with, and worse, this person was the father of her child. How stupid she had been, she thought, glancing towards the door hoping for someone to arrive with good news.

Finally, tired from the day and the tension during the evening, Thea fell into a restless sleep. Nightmare after nightmare haunted her until she finally woke up drenched in sweat. She had only slept for three hours, and the nightmares left her feeling much more tired than before she fell asleep.

Thea took a shower, hoping to freshen up, but the effect was only temporary. Finally, she decided that it was better to be among people and went downstairs, where Koev and his team were trying to locate Georgi.

'Did you find him?' she asked.

'No. He disappeared and covered his tracks. According to Popov, Georgi went five minutes after him to the police station, and after seeing that you were gone, he left. No one has seen him since, and his personal phone has no signal. We don't know where he is. Georgi didn't go to the house or the usual places. It looks like he left town right away.'

'You're unlikely to find him,' Thea said.

'Come with me to my office. I would like to talk to you,' Koev said and headed there. Thea followed him. After they were both settled, Koev sighed and looked at her with concern. 'Thea, I want to be honest with you and tell you what awaits you from now on.'

'In what sense, what awaits me?'

'You know you can't stay here for long. Mary and I will find you a job and a place to live.'

'I don't want a job and accommodation! I want to find my daughter.'

'Let me finish. I'm hoping today we can decode the laptop and find some information that will lead us to where she is. The problem is that we think Georgi will find your daughter before us and try to find you through her. He'll probably be waiting for you where she lives. He's a maniac, Thea, and he'll haunt you until the end. Maria will be his trump card. He'll hold her until he finds you. She'll be safe until he finds you. If you go there, you'll both be in trouble. Leave it to us to find her and bring her back to you.'

'I can't stand and wait. This is going to drive me crazy.'

'I am asking you to think before you decide what you're going to do. If you want us to tell you where she is when we find her, we will comply with your request and tell you. Our practice is not to, but you've helped us a lot. But I advise you, if we find out where Maria is, not to go there. You'll put both of you in danger.'

'Okay. I'll think about it.'

'In the meantime, as I already told you, we will find you accommodation and a job.'

'Okay,' she agreed, tears welling up in her eyes. Thea felt helpless. She had expected to find her daughter quickly. The reality that the search would take time and that Georgi would take advantage of Maria shocked her. She had unwittingly put her daughter in his sights. How had she not thought of that before? How naive and stupid she was.

'Relax. Everything will be fine.' Koev tried to calm her down, but Thea was crying and her whole body was shaking. He walked up to her and put his arm around her shoulder. He didn't know what to say to her.

A little while later, Mary called them into the meeting room.

'We managed to download the information from the laptop. It will take time for us to read every email and go through all the files, but we found a folder of addresses and names. Unfortunately, most are out of the country. We're guessing that's where the kids were taken, but we need to check first to be sure. Our colleagues called the police to send officers on duty to the addresses in Sofia. We'll know who lives there within an hour.'

'Are there any dates?' Thea asked.

'No. Addresses and first names only. Nothing else. It is possible that even the names are not real. Now we just have to wait. Let's hope that our colleagues will act quickly.'

For Thea, the wait was excruciating. Every time she saw Mary or Koev talking on the phone, she hoped for some news, but in most cases, they just shook their heads slightly. There was no news for two hours. Finally, Koev and Mary gathered everyone working on the case and asked Thea to join them.

'The police checked most of the addresses in Sofia. They all report the same thing. The houses are empty. The parents called the school and picked up the children yesterday as an emergency. No one has seen them since. We are too late,' Koev said and looked Thea straight in the eyes. Thea's heart seemed to break in two. Georgi had warned everyone that the police knew their whereabouts and now the information they had was useless.

'I know the news is not good, but we still have a lead. We know who the adoptive parents are, but I still don't know who the children are. From this point on, we will question anyone who has spoken to them. I hope that by getting the descriptions of the children from kindergartens, schools, neighbours, doctors, and anyone who would have come into contact with them, we will find out which child lived at which address.'

'How many addresses and names did you find?' Thea asked.

'We found 108. More than we expected.'

'What, 108?' Thea repeated, the despair evident in her voice. 'How many of them are located outside the country?'

'It's 103,' answered Mary. 'Most addresses are in Greece, but the rest are scattered throughout Europe. We will seek the help of our colleagues there. We have already started the procedure.'

'It's going to be too late, isn't it? Did they have enough time to move the kids?'

'We think so, Thea, but they may not have been able to contact them, and the children may still be there.'

Where is Maria? Thea wondered. Had Georgi left her nearby or sent her as far away as possible?

After the meeting ended, Koev again called Thea to his office.

'What did you decide?'

'I'll look for her. I can't sit in some room or work without knowing where she is.'

'Thea, I can't include you in the investigation. You didn't even have to attend that meeting.'

'I can't stay away!' shouted Thea, and her cry made Koev jump a little.

'Give us time to find out where Maria is, and I promise you that you will be the first to know where she is. Now calm down. I understand that you are under pressure, but my colleagues and I, as you can see, are doing everything possible to find each and every one of these children. You heard Mary, 108 of them are out there somewhere, including your Maria. Let us do our job.'

'Why don't you give this information to the media? Maybe you will find the children through them faster.'

'In my opinion, this will scare the people who are holding these children and force them to hide deeper. If they hide, it will take us more time to find them.'

Thea felt sick again. She didn't want to stop looking for her daughter, she wanted to be part of the process. However, what Koev said made her think, and finally she agreed to accept the job and the accommodation.

'I promise to keep you informed,' the lieutenant told her. Then he asked a colleague to drive Thea to her new place and help her settle in and introduce herself to the factory where she was supposed to work.

'You will have two days to calm down and rest before starting work,' Mary told her. 'In one box, we have prepared everything you will need to get started. We've opened a bank account in your name, but you'll also be given cash when you leave the building. In the room where you will be accommodated, you will find a phone and a laptop. My phone number and Koev's will be saved. You can call us at any time, but keep in mind that we may not be able to answer right away. If you need anything else just let us know.'

'Will I live alone?'

'No, there will be three more women. I want to warn you that the investigation may take longer than we think, and it is important for you to not share any information with anyone, not even the women you will be living with temporarily.'

'Okay,' Thea agreed and reluctantly headed for the elevator.

'Thea,' Mary called, 'before you leave, I wanted to tell you that without you we wouldn't have succeeded.'

'That's not true. We both know you would have succeeded without me sooner or later.'

'Koev has been working on this case for many years. You have no idea how disappointed he is in himself for not finding out about the other kids. He is very impressed with you and the work you have done.'

'Well, but now he's sending me away as a thank-you, isn't he?' said Thea. Without saying anything else, she entered the elevator and left Mary silent in front of the elevator. On the ground floor, one of the employees put Thea in a car and drove her to the flat where she was supposed to live.

The women Thea met there were of different ages and with different personal stories. Two of them were smiling, with a glint of hope in their eyes. The third was timid and restless. Thea was used to living with many people, and the presence of the other women did not bother her. On the very first day, she managed to make friends with everyone, and although she was angry and worried, she managed to control her bad mood and not convey it to her roommates.

Koev did not call her the first day; he only wrote that they were working hard and if he learned something, he would call her.

Alone with her thoughts in the small room, Thea tried to dream. She imagined the day when she would see Maria again. She dreamed of renting a flat and getting a job, probably something that she could do from a laptop. A job that wouldn't keep her away from her daughter. Thea couldn't imagine leaving Maria alone or having someone else take care of her. The mere thought that she might soon be found warmed her, but the worry that Georgi had probably found her and was going to use her as a bargaining chip chilled her blood. The more Thea thought, the more her worry grew, and the lack of information from Koev's team drove her even more crazy. Finally, Thea realized that every time she got up, her knees were shaking with tension, and it was as if her arms couldn't find a place.

Trapped, she tried to calm herself with music, then borrowed one of the books from the library in the living room. When that didn't help either, Thea decided to take a walk in the small park near the building where she lived. The warm wind and contemplation of the water in the small lake in the park finally calmed her down. A fountain had been built by the lake, and the sound of the water flowing from it seemed to calm her nerves even more. *Everything will be all right*, she reassured herself, and for the first time in a long time, she fell asleep and did not wake all night.

The next day, however, things got complicated. Thea woke up to a commotion in the kitchen. Two of the women had fought, and the third was trying to break them up.

'What is going on here?' shouted Thea and this caused everyone to turn to her.

'She took my dress,' said one of them.

'I did not. I bought this dress two days ago.'

The battle between the two began again.

'How much money does the dress cost?' Thea shouted again.

'It was a gift for me,' said one woman, and the other mentioned the price. Thea went to her room, took that amount from the woman, and left it on the table.

'Here, buy a new one. Now let me rest!' Thea said and turned her back on them, going back to her room.

'She's crazy,' she heard one of the women say, but Thea ignored her. There was silence in the flat, and that was what she needed. The opinions of strangers did not interest her. Unfortunately, the scandals between her roommates continued and became more and more violent.

Finally, Thea couldn't stand it and called Koev. 'It's worse here than in the hamlet.'

'You're telling me?' He laughed. 'We are trying to calm them down, but we can't.'

'Can you move me somewhere else?'

'I will try to find you a better place,' he promised.

'Thanks. How is the investigation going?'

'I was planning on calling you a little later, but you beat me to it. We found two of the children.'

'When?'

'This morning.'

'Where did you find them?'

'Not far from here, in a village close to Sofia.'

'But you won't tell me which village?'

'No, it's better not to know. We are still looking for the other kids. Unfortunately, we have no information on Maria's whereabouts, but I hope to find her soon.'

'If you don't find her within two weeks, I will start looking for her myself.'

'We'll find her, Thea. Give me some more time.'

However, Thea did not want to give any more time. She started having nightmares again every night and woke up in a sweat. Sometimes she dreamed that Georgi was kissing her baby, other times that he was taking her with him. The unknown was driving her crazy and she felt like she had to do something. She needed action and a place where she could gather her thoughts. Maybe she knew something that would help her find Maria. Thea thought more and more about the two men who had met at the Blue Café. Her intuition told her that they were an important part of the investigation, but Koev and Mary were never able to find them. Thea's description did not match any suspect. They had hit a snag with this trail. However, Thea thought someone should have gone and spoken to the café owner. It was the first thing Thea would do if Koev and his team hadn't found her daughter in two weeks.

9

Lieutenant Koev kept his promise and moved Thea to another place. This time she shared a flat with two other women who, like her, sought solitude and peace. All three were more often in front of the laptops than in front of the TV and hardly spoke to each other. The calm environment worked well for Thea. Every two days, Koev or Mary called her and gave her fragmentary information about the case. In just one week, they had managed to find another forty children. Koev was pleased, even smiling, something that was rare for him. However, Thea continued to grieve, and at the beginning of the second week, she began to search the internet for information about cases similar to hers. As she had expected, she wasn't the only one whose child was taken by force. However, in the majority of cases, the children were never found, especially those who were taken abroad. Her idea to publicize her case quickly died after realizing how often the children and their illegal adoptive parents were found dead after such a step. This was how the sellers covered their tracks. Koev was right, only the media would gain from this, so Thea abandoned this plan.

The other thing Thea researched was Georgi's ex-wife. There was no way that woman didn't hear or see something. Thea wanted to find her and talk to her face-to-face. She would threaten her life if she had to, but she would learn everything Georgi's ex-wife knew about Maria. Koev and Mary said they had questioned her several times, but each time Laura denied knowing anything about the deals. Thea knew from living in Georgi's house only briefly that Georgi's ex-wife was lying. And she was lying because she was more afraid of Georgi than of the police. If Thea could find out where she had moved to live with the children, she would go and talk to her. But how would she find out? Koev and Mary refused to give her the information.

Thea had several ideas on how to continue the search for her daughter on her own, and in her free time she thought only of this. Finding Maria was her priority; what she hadn't guessed, and never considered, though, was that her own mother had now found herself in her situation. Kina had contacted the police and declared Thea missing. On this occasion, Koev called Thea one morning and told her that she urgently needed to go to his office.

'Your mother went to Georgi's house several times to look for you, and after a week of not being able to contact you, she went to the police. Fortunately, Popov was on duty then and promised to look for you. According to him, she looked devastated and thought that Georgi had killed you.'

'Maybe I should have told her somehow that I am fine.'

'We thought you two weren't close. According to your testimony, she herself gave her grandchild to the couple who took her.'

'That's how it was. But I think she regretted it later. I didn't think ...' Thea cried. What her mother had been through in recent weeks.

'Thea, I called you here because she wants to meet you.'

'Really? Is she here?'

'No, she's not here. I wanted to talk to you first to make sure you agree to the meeting. In my opinion, she will not stop looking for you, and you should go and talk to her. You have to calm her down, but at the same time, you have to be very careful. She may have been sent by your brother and father, though we don't think so. We don't think Georgi forced her to find you. Whatever the reason is, it's best you meet her.'

'Where is the meeting?'

'In a café in the centre. Our colleagues will take you there and then return you to your accommodation.'

'Okay. When should I meet her?'

'Now. She's waiting for you there.'

Thea got up, and Koev called two of his colleagues to accompany her to the café. As she rode in the back seat, Thea thought about her mother and her hard life. However, she wondered whether to believe her, whether to trust her after so many years of cold treatment. Her mother always did what her father asked. Had she been sent by him this time, or had a mother's love proved to be stronger? Thea was asking herself all these questions and looking out the window at the passing cars. When they arrived and entered the almost-empty café, Thea realized that Popov had been right. The woman sitting with trembling hands in her lap was a pale copy of Kina. There were bags under her eyes, her mouth trembled slightly, and her eyes betrayed such obvious grief that it was impossible for those around her not to feel it. When Kina finally looked up and saw Thea, tears welled up in her sad, big, black eyes. The emotion seemed to be unleashed, and the woman's body shook with her crying.

'I thought you were dead!' Kina cried and pressed her daughter tightly to her.

'I'm not, Mom. Look at me, I'm here,' Thea whispered and cried too. Kina continued to hold her tightly and sob.

'Where were you? Why didn't you call me?' she asked.

'I was looking for my daughter,' Thea answered.

'She is far away. I shouldn't have given her to them,' Kina continued to cry. 'It's my fault. I should have stopped them.'

'There was no way you could stop them, Mom.' Thea tried to calm her down, but in her heart, she still couldn't forgive her.

Kina finally let her go and sat in the chair.

'Did you manage to find her?'

'No. I'm still looking for her. Do you know anything that can help me?' Thea whispered.

'I wish I knew. Georgi didn't tell us anything. He has also disappeared.'

'I know.'

'Is he with you?'

'No, Mom, he's not with me. If he finds me, he won't leave me alive, so it's important that you don't tell anyone that you saw me. To nobody, do you understand?'

'Yes. I understand. He's a dangerous man, Thea. You always knew it and you went with him anyway.'

'I left because I wanted to find out where Maria was.'

'Who is Maria?'

'My daughter – that's what I called her.'

'You chose a nice name for her. You should have told me you called her that.'

'I should have, but I didn't know if I could trust you.'

'I know, I wasn't a good mother. Mrs. Mariola would have taken better care of you.'

'Don't think about it now. The past is in the past, you can't change it.'

'That's right,' said Kina and sobbed again.

Koev's colleague signalled to Thea that they should go.

'Don't tell anyone you saw me, Mom. Do you promise?'

'I promise. But you promise to tell me when you find her.'

'Okay. I'll find a way to let you know when I find her.'

The two women embraced, and Thea headed for the car. The moment she opened the door of the café, three men approached and pulled her out. Everything happened so quickly that Koev's colleagues were unable to react. One of the men locked the door of the café and blocked their way out, while the other two put Thea into a car and pushed her into the back seat. She tried to look out the window to see if anyone was coming to help her, but all she saw was her mother's terrified face. Someone had followed Kina. The car drove off, and one of the men was pressing Thea roughly and forcing her to lie down in the back seat. Realizing what was happening, she tried to free herself from his grip and open the car door, but the door was locked.

God help me, she thought, and began to pray for someone to save her. The car was moving fast and making many turns. After about an hour, it finally stopped. The man sitting next to her in the back seat made her get up and go outside. Then he directed her to walk towards an old building. Thea looked around, wanted to call for help, but after seeing where they were, decided there was no point. There were only half-demolished old factories around. It was unlikely there would be anyone there to help her. As she entered the building, Thea smelled smoke and a strange smell. Something was burning; she could even feel the heat. She slowed, but the man behind her nudged her and forced her forward. Georgi was sitting on an old chair and throwing objects into a large fireplace. When he saw her, he smiled.

'Welcome,' he said and pointed to a chair for her to sit down. Thea didn't answer. Instead, she looked around. The room was large and almost empty. Only in one corner was set aside a sort of small office with a desk, computer, and printer. The floor was dusty, and she could see the dust rising from the sunlight coming in from the small windows. There was something dark about this building, and despite the warmth coming from the fireplace, Thea shivered.

'Do you like my new house?' asked Georgi. Thea was silent, and that made him nervous. He got up slowly from the chair, pushed it aside, and approached her. With a quick gesture, Georgi grabbed her face and forced her to look into his eyes.

'I like the old one better,' she finally said, trying to look away.

'If you liked it, you wouldn't run away, don't you think?'

Thea didn't answer. Georgi's pressure was causing her pain. She tried to free herself, but he gripped her even tighter and forced her into the chair.

'Why?' he shouted. 'Why did you leave? I gave you everything, did everything you wanted!'

'I wanted you to return my daughter, but you didn't,' she said quietly.

'This kid was going to get in our way. I never wanted it, and you know it. I only wanted you.'

Georgi spoke calmly, as if he were talking to a friend.

'Will you tell me where she is?'

'No. She is the reason we are here now. I hate this kid, and if I find it ...'

Georgi's voice rose, and Thea felt his hatred for Maria. *No child deserves a father like that,* she thought.

'Why am I here?' she asked.

'This is your new home. We'll live here until it's time to move.'

Thea looked at him in surprise. 'After everything I've done, you still want to live with me?'

'Wouldn't that be the worst punishment for you?' He smiled at her with that thin smile he gave his clients when they realized they had made a big mistake.

Thea was horrified at the thought of spending days and nights with him.

'Why me? You can have any other.'

'Anyone else, but not you. I love a challenge, Thea, you must have figured that out by now. I can assure you that there is no escape from here. The area is remote, and I will always be with you. I will not go anywhere. I have people I pay to do my work. Now I think of myself as a retired person who has decided to enjoy life and spend time with his beautiful young wife. When all the documents are ready, we will even go on vacation as a family.'

'You thought of everything, huh!'

'That's right. To the smallest detail, remember this.'

Georgi got up, put more wood in the fireplace, and this time Thea realized what that smell was that she had smelled at the entrance. The smell was of roasting. Her hair stood on end as she realized what was in the fire. Or more precisely, who was baking there. The heat and disgust made her sick and she slowly collapsed to the floor.

When she recovered and opened her eyes, she met Georgi's gaze.

'Did we agree that you take your pills regularly? You're not pregnant, are you?' he asked with reproach in his eyes.

'I am not pregnant,' she said, but did not dare to tell him why she had lost consciousness.

'Okay. Supper is ready. Change and go downstairs.'

Thea nodded, waited for him to leave the room, and looked around. The windows were barred, and she wasn't surprised by that. In the closet were her clothes and slippers. There were no shoes. Everything was folded and arranged carefully. Next to her closet was a smaller one with a few shirts and jeans that he wore. Georgi had indeed planned to live with her and keep her as a prisoner. At least for the moment, he clearly had no intention of killing her, but the smell from the fireplace still made Thea tremble with fear. Georgi was crazy and unpredictable, and who knows what feelings he would have for her tomorrow. Maybe he wouldn't be so in love. She had to find a way to keep challenging him. The moment she became uninterested in him, Thea knew that she would follow the fate of the poor man in the fire. She changed and deliberately delayed a few minutes before going down to him. Thea knew it would make him angry, but now she knew how to play the game so that she would stay alive longer. She hoped Koev and his colleagues would find some kind of trail and find her.

When she went down to Georgi, he was alone. A small table was placed in the right corner of the room, and a cart with various dishes of food was placed on the side.

'Sit down,' he said when he saw her, and she sat down on the chair opposite him. 'As you can see there is no equipped kitchen here, so one of my men will deliver food to us three times a day.'

Thea looked around again.

'What is this building?' she asked to distract the attention from herself.

'This is a former glass factory. Ten years ago, some of the most beautiful glass Christmas toys in Europe were made here.'

'So, that's why there are all these big fireplaces?'

'They are called furnaces. Yes, in these furnaces the craftsmen melted the glass until it turned into liquid. I have found another use for them. I think you can guess what it is, but I thought I'd tell you anyway.'

'You can save that detail. I don't want to know what you're doing.'

'We will be spending a lot of time together, so it is good to know what is going on in our family home.'

Thea swallowed hard. He really imagined they were family.

'Okay, tell me what happened today,' she said quietly and pushed the plate of food aside. Georgi continued to eat and gestured with his finger for her to continue. She shook her head.

'You don't want to eat, okay. But you'll have to listen to me. This will be one of your duties. Let me tell you what happened today. Remember the elderly couple who came to pick up your child?'

'Yes.'

'I didn't expect you to go and see your mother today. I thought you two didn't get along. That's why I called Sonya and Petko. I wanted to know where they took the child.'

'You didn't know where she was?' Thea was surprised.

'I knew but imagine my surprise when I went to the address, I gave them and the child was not there. I knew you would keep looking for your baby, and

I wanted to be prepared when you found it. But it wasn't there and never had been.'

'What?' shouted Thea in surprise. 'How come she was never there? Where did they take her?'

'They sold your child to another family who paid more money and took the difference. Can you imagine they tried to screw me? Me?'

'Where is she now? Is she okay?'

Georgi slammed his fist on the table, and the dishes bounced and made a jingling sound. Thea also jumped in fright.

'This child is not important. Stop asking where she is! I am the important one in this case. They tried to make a fool of me.'

Thea nodded and tried to calm herself. However, thousands of questions were running through her head. Where had they taken Maria? If Georgi didn't know where she was, how would she find her?

Georgi began to eat again, and he watched her carefully.

'They took advantage of the deal.'

'And you killed them and put them in the furnace.'

'Only him, I sent her with one of my people to find the baby and return it to its real parents.'

'We are her real parents,' said Thea and immediately regretted her words. Georgi got up, approached her and taking her by the elbow, made her rise from the chair. Then he pulled her to her feet and forced her to look into his eyes.

'If you repeat that one more time, you will follow the fate of Petko.'

He was whispering, and Thea could feel his malice and anger as the words seemed to come out through his clenched teeth. She nodded her understanding and sat down at the table pretending to eat. Thea wanted to calm him down and keep him talking. However, he walked away and just then his phone rang, startling them both.

'Yes. What? How did they know she was here? Do what you can to hold them back.'

Then Georgi turned to her. 'Your friends quickly found us. I expected it to take them at least a day or two.'

He walked over to Thea, took her hand, and pulled her up the stairs. She tried to free herself, but he gripped her even tighter, and Thea screamed in pain.

'I can't understand why you resist. Don't you think I haven't made a plan how to get out of here if something happens?'

She didn't answer. He pulled her into a closet-sized room with many things inside. Thea looked around, and while Georgi was trying to move something that had fallen to the floor, she picked up an iron rod that was near her and pressed it to her body. Georgi tried to close the door, and when he turned his back on her, she hit him on the head with all her might. This stunned him and gave her time to get out. Thea ran towards the front door, but one of Georgi's men stopped her and grabbed her by the waist. She screamed, tried to free herself, but the man had a firm grip on her and wouldn't let go. When she already thought that she would not be able to free herself, someone hit him hard, and he collapsed at her feet.

'Everything is fine,' one of Koev's colleagues told her.

'There, in that little room,' Thea said and started towards the exit. When she came out of the iron gate, she saw a large part of the lieutenant's team. Koev himself was nowhere to be seen, but Mary was nearby.

'How did you find me?' Thea asked as she tried to take a deep breath.

'We had a second team on the street in front of the café. It took them longer than we expected to figure out exactly which building they brought you to, which is why we were so late. I'm glad you're alive, Thea. That smell …'

'I know exactly who it's from.'

'Okay,' Mary said and helped Thea into the car.

'Where is Koev?'

'Inside the building. I guess he'll stay there until he gathers all the evidence.'

Thea was about to ask something else, but Georgi's exit from the old factory drew her attention. He was watching her too. There was a glint in his eyes that scared her.

'We will talk to him,' said Mary. 'We'll force him to tell us where your daughter is.'

'He doesn't know where she is,' Thea whispered softly, and tears began to flow from her eyes.

10

Koev and his team interrogated Georgi for three days. However, he refused to talk to them. The only person he wanted to talk to was Thea. She agreed to talk to him at first but then gave up on the idea.

'He won't tell me anything. He'll just play tricks on me.'

At the end of the third day, everyone had gathered in the meeting room on the fourth floor of the building and discussed their next course of action. After Georgi was arrested, several charges were brought against him and his closest people as well. It turned out that Thea's family had taken a large part in what Georgi called deals, and they, like him, were in custody. None of them wanted to talk or testify. Georgi had promised them protection, had hired lawyers, and with that he kept them quiet. In addition to her brother, mother, and father, some of her neighbours were also taken into custody. Benny and her husband, Boyan, had also been questioned. After the interrogation, the pregnant woman stayed to talk to Thea.

'Chaos reigns in the hamlet,' she said. 'Everyone blames you for betraying us.'

'Didn't they betray me, Benny? They all allowed my daughter to be taken. Then they wanted to beat me to death because I dared to look for her.'

'Thea, you must return to the hamlet. You owe it to the people who live there.'

'What I need to do is find my daughter. You will manage without me.'

Benny tried to get her to promise to go her back to her father's house, but Thea was adamant. She had been born there, she grew up there, but she wasn't going to raise her child in that place.

'At least say who you think can temporarily take your father's place.'

'Maybe Boyan will manage,' offered Thea and let the pregnant woman think about it.

When Benny left Thea visited her mother in the detention centre. Although she regretted what had happened, Kina had participated in the child trafficking, and Koev would not forgive her for that. Neither did Thea.

Kina had refused to help them in any way. All she kept saying was that she was sorry for what had happened, and that Thea should do everything she could to find Maria. But there was no sign of Maria. The police had declared Sonya a nationally wanted person. Georgi's arrest was announced in the news, and Sonya had probably found out that he was no longer at large. However, Sonya's inclusion on the wanted list was not announced to the media. Koev and his team assumed that if her name and face came out, most of the 'adopters' would cover their tracks, and finding the children would become even more difficult.

'She is the only one who has information about the adoptive parents,' said Koev to those gathered in the meeting hall. 'Finding her is our priority. Sonya knows not only where Maria is, but also the other children.'

'Do we know who the man was with her?'

'We don't know his name, but we have a description of him from the men who worked with him. According to them, they went to some village near the Black Sea, but we do not know if they arrived there. They may still be nearby and hiding.'

'Did you ask Georgi if he knows where they live?'

'As you know, he refuses to talk to us,' Koev said, and unconsciously his eyes turned to Thea, who was sitting at a desk in the large office. She was not present at the meeting but could be seen from the hall window. Sensing his gaze, Thea turned and stared at him.

'We have to make her talk to him,' he whispered and released everyone present at the meeting. Then, leaving the meeting room, Koev headed towards her. 'We need to talk,' he told her and gestured to the door of his office.

She got up and headed there. 'What's wrong? Did you learn something new?'

'No. We've been going in circles for days.'

'What do you want to talk about?' she asked and sat down in the chair across from him.

'I would like to talk about you and Georgi.'

Thea leaned back and sighed.

'I have told you everything I know, and I am doing my best ...'

'You're not doing your best,' he interrupted her. 'And you know I'm right. You should talk to him.'

'He will only play with us and won't tell me anything.'

'You should try to play his game and extract information. You are smart and you know him better than any of us, Thea. You know how to play by his rules. Only you can find out where Sonya lives, and perhaps where she is now. I guess Georgi has his sources in custody and still receives news from the outside world.'

Thea tried to protest as Koev spoke, but his last words made her think twice.

'Maybe you're right and he knows where she is. Maybe he already knows where Maria is. I will talk to him.'

'Good,' sighed a relieved Koev. 'Tell me when you are ready, and I will accompany you.'

Thea needed to prepare emotionally for the meeting with Georgi, so she decided to go out and take a walk in the nearby park. It was a nice day; people were out with their kids and pets and walking around mostly smiling. This was the life she longed for. To have a home, to have a job, and to take care of her daughter. To take her to school in the morning and spend her free time with her. She didn't dream of anything else. Georgi and her family had taken that dream away from her. The hatred she had begun to feel for him was burning her inside. And the fire from within had blackened her thoughts, had taken over her body, and in her veins, her blood seemed no longer to flow. Thea felt that this dark feeling could no longer be hidden, and Georgi would feel her hatred for him. He would see it in her eyes, so Thea had to find a way to hide it.

'Here you are.' She heard Koev's voice.

'Yes, I need to walk alone and get some fresh air.' Thea didn't want to talk to him right now.

'Are you teasing me?' he asked.

'Yes,' she admitted.

'And what if I suggest we talk this time as friends?'

'I don't think we can talk like friends because we're not like that,' she said.

'You're right. And what about as people, with a not particularly pleasant start in life?'

Thea was silent. She had thought about Koev sometimes and his obsession with working around the clock to find missing people. Someone on his team had mentioned to her that he was like this because of childhood experiences.

'How hard was your start on a scale of one to ten?' she asked.

'Nine,' he said, and Thea saw him swallow hard.

'And why do you want to talk to me about this?'

'Because I see the look in your eyes. The hatred in your eyes when we mention Georgi's name.'

'You noticed.'

'Yes, I did. This is exactly how I felt many years ago, so I recognise the symptoms.'

'And what is the treatment, according to you?'

'I'm not a doctor, and I don't know, but I can tell you what happened to me. It's been many years, and I haven't told anyone until now. I hadn't met anyone who I thought would be able to understand me.'

'How old were you? '

'I was fourteen when I felt that I hated my adoptive parents so much that I wanted to kill them. So, I did my best to get out of there and never come back. But this feeling stayed with me for many years, and now I regret that I didn't do something sooner to stop it from taking hold of me.'

'What do you think you should have done?'

'I should have, when I had the opportunity, faced them and told them how I felt.'

'Why don't you do it now?'

'Because they're dead. When I felt ready to do it, it turned out that they were no longer there. I was too late. I don't want you to go through the same thing, Thea. You are young, you have a lot of time and life ahead of you. That's why I advise you to stand before him now and do the right thing. To do what your intuition tells you.'

'And why do you think this will help me?'

'I have read a lot about this. You need to emotionally free yourself from this person. If you don't do it now, in a year or two it will be too late.'

Thea and Koev moved among the crowd. She was so lost in their conversation that sometimes she bumped into people, then with a blank look she apologized to them and continued walking. Something in Koev's words had sobered her up, and the black veil that had appeared in front of her eyes for several weeks seemed to lift.

'Only he can help us find all the children, right?'

'No, Thea, only *you* can help us. You are the key to the puzzle. He is the door you have to open.'

She walked for a while longer, then turned and headed in the direction of the office. Koev sighed in relief and followed her.

11

Two hours later, Thea was in the detention centre, waiting for Koev to complete the formalities surrounding their visit. As she waited, she saw the lawyer who had been hired by Georgi for herself and her family. It was strange to Thea because he had paid for their defence. For the rest of the people from the hamlet involved in the case, he had not made this gesture. Maybe Georgi wanted to take advantage of her family again, or maybe he hoped to keep them quiet. Whatever his reason, the lawyer was unlikely to help any of them. The evidence against everyone involved in child trafficking was overwhelming, and the testimony was increasing every day.

To Thea's surprise, her entire family were involved, all of her siblings. This further emphasized the moral differences she had with her family. Perhaps sensing that her conscience would not accept such a crime, her parents had kept her away from it. According to some people in the hamlet, it was her mother who wanted to keep Thea's hands and criminal record clean. One of Kina's neighbours had met Thea briefly and told her that her mother wanted her daughter to have a different life, a better future.

'Your infatuation with Georgi disappointed her a lot. It's like you stabbed her in the heart. I think the fact that the child was his meant that she agreed to let him get rid of it. Then, of course, she regretted her actions and kept crying, but it was too late.'

The neighbour's story surprised Thea a lot. She had always thought that she was part of the family, that she knew everything about them, but now it became clear to her that this was not the case. They hid their crimes from her because they couldn't trust her. Thea had always felt different, and they had felt the same about her. She still didn't know the full story and which of them was involved in what exactly. She didn't know the details because the investigators weren't allowed to tell her those, but from what she heard from the other people around her, she knew that after their trial, they would all probably to go to prison for several years. She would be left without a family. Her nephews were already being taken care of by other relatives, and no one wanted to entrust her with their care. Everyone hated her. Thea had been left alone and the feeling of loneliness had intensified in the last few hours, especially after her conversation with Koev.

The heavy iron door leading to Georgi's cell opened and startled her. Koev stood before her, looked at her questioningly, and after she nodded, he let her go inside. The cell was smaller than she had expected. Inside there was a bed, a table, and a chair, also a shelf with two books. Everything inside was painted metallic grey. This colour made her feel cold. She stepped forward and stared at the chair in front of her.

Georgi was tied to the bed on which he was sitting and watching her with shining eyes.

'I was convinced that in the end you would come to see me. Why are you so late? Is this the one who didn't let you visit me?'

Georgi was talking about Koev but did not look at him. His eyes followed Thea's every move. As she crossed the cell and sat in the chair, he studied her. He had stared at her face at first, obviously expecting her to meet his eyes, but she walked with her head down. Then he scanned her body, first her ankles, then he seemed to feel the rest of her with his eyes. Finally, his gaze settled on her lips and as he looked at them, he unconsciously licked his own.

Koev had stood aside and watched his reaction. Before he put Thea in the cell, he thought everything would go according to plan, but now he doubted it. She did not dare to look at Georgi, probably to hide her hatred for him. Georgi, for his part, had become nervous at her presence. Koev could see his fingers trembling. His lips had stretched into a nervous smile, and his eyes had darkened. The glint in them startled him. Koev was frightened by the wildness in Georgi's eyes. It was as if a feral animal had seen its victim. However, Koev could not judge whether this glow was from love or from hatred. It could be a mixture of both, he thought, and he motioned for the guard to come closer. His intuition told him that he might need the guard's help.

'Won't you answer my questions?' asked Georgi, breaking the painful silence that was in the room.

Thea looked up and met his eyes. A shudder ran through her body, and she unconsciously pulled back. Then she grabbed the back of the chair and tried to get up.

'Don't leave,' Georgi said, anticipating her intention to get up and turn her back on him.

'Why?' she asked as she got up from her chair.

"Don't leave.' He hit the iron table that separated them with his hand. Thea was now standing with her back to him, and the impact shook her whole body. Without turning to Georgi, she approached Koev, whispered something in his ear and left the cell. As expected, Georgi freaked out and started shouting after her, insulting her, then begging her, but she never came back to him. Koev and the guard locked the door of his cell and left him to cry.

'You should have stayed and tried to talk to him,' Koev scolded Thea after catching up with her in the corridor.

'No, I shouldn't have. You told me to play his game, and I did. Georgi does not like easy victories; over time I understood that. He needs a challenge and for him to tell me what I want, I will have to give him that challenge.'

'Thea, you think you know him well, but you don't. Georgi can wrap you around his little finger if you go to him too often.'

'Just a few hours ago, you told me that I was the only one who could make him sing.'

'And I still believe it. But ...'

'I know Georgi very well, so please let me do what I have to do. Let me play his game, and you'll see it pay off.'

'Okay,' Koev agreed after a short hesitation. 'I hope I don't regret it.'

'Me too,' said Thea.

Actually, Thea had no intention of leaving so quickly, but Georgi's look, that madness in his eyes, had scared her. She needed time to recover; she had to leave quickly so that Georgi would not feel her fear.

Thea was left trembling as she walked to her quarters; she squeezed her palms tightly. When she entered the empty apartment, she lay down on the living room sofa and cried. Despair overwhelmed her. She didn't have the strength to stand in front of Georgi. She hated him. She hated him so much that she wanted to hurt him. What a paradox; she wanted to destroy him, she didn't want to meet his eyes anymore, and he was the only one who could help her find Maria. And that look, that madness, would that be passed down genetically to her daughter? This man was crazy, and Thea had known it for a long time, but only now did she truly feel the intensity of his madness.

At today's meeting, a veil was lifted in front of her eyes, and she saw everything more clearly, but instead of calming her, this clarity nudged her in another direction. For the first time in her life, Thea felt real fear and terror. Until now, she had always had the feeling that she would find a loophole and get out of any mess, but today, after seeing his look, she realized that Georgi would never leave her. He would haunt her and her daughter for the rest of his life. Now Thea saw this fanaticism, this bad trait in his character.

He was born this way; she was convinced of that. A difficult childhood was not to blame for his character. But Georgi had learned how to hide it. Thea had to mentally prepare for their next meeting. She had to resist his gaze and find a way to get him to talk, to get him to trust her again, to start sharing with her and telling her about his childhood, his projects and if she was lucky enough to trick him into telling her about Sonya.

Sonya and her companion seemed to have sunk to the bottom of the earth. No one had seen or heard from them since they left the glass factory, and Thea was worried that Georgi had lied to her. Maybe he hadn't sent her to find Maria; maybe he'd had his man liquidate her somewhere else.

There were many worries in Thea's head. She sighed, got up from the sofa, and searched her bag for her phone. She had to call Koev and ask him to arrange another meeting with Georgi the next day. There was no point in delaying; the sooner she was done with this psychopath, the better.

Koev did not agree to a meeting the next day.

'Better wait. Georgi is furious. He is mad. He has been screaming and throwing everything in his cell against the walls and floor.'

'Maybe my visit will calm him down.'

'I've been doing this for many years, Thea, and I know when a person is dangerous to himself and others. He can't bear the thought of being in that cell and you not being around him. Let him become tamer and we'll go again.'

'And if he doesn't become tame?'

'Then we will have to move him to a ward with a medical staff. Today they tried to give him sedatives with his water, but as far as I know, he didn't drink much. I think if we give him time, he will calm down. You need a break too. How long is it since you have slept well?'

'Since Georgi kidnapped me, I haven't been able to sleep well. I keep dreaming of that furnace and the crackling body inside.' Thea frowned and wrinkled her nose as she spoke; she could still smell it.

'Rest tonight, watch TV or read a book.'

'Yes, I will do it. Koev, there were two books on the shelf in the cell. Do you happen to know which they are?'

'I don't know, but I can have the prison guard check.'

'Text me when you find out. I'm interested in what Georgi is reading. It's hardly fiction.'

'Okay, I'll text you when I find out. Now calm down and rest.'

'See you tomorrow, Koev.'

'See you tomorrow.'

Thea retired to her room and was just about to try to relax and rest when the doorbell rang. She hadn't heard the doorbell ring since she'd been in this flat. Thea and her roommates did not receive guests, nor did they buy anything to be delivered by courier. They had agreed from the beginning that none of them would reveal their identities in any way because the people they were involved with were dangerous. Therefore, when she heard the bell ring, Thea was worried and stayed in her room, trying not to move and even to breathe.

'Thea, open it,' she heard a familiar voice, but her brain refused to associate the voice with a face, and she did not move. 'Thea, I know you're in. I saw you come in. Open up, I have something to tell you.'

Thea continued to stand in the room and try to remember where she knew the voice from.

'Open it, it's urgent. My fellow reporter happened to come across something interesting.'

Only now did Thea remember whose voice it was. She went to the door and looked through the peephole to make sure she was right.

'Bobby? How did you find me?' She was surprised and opened the door wide for him to enter the apartment.

'I have my sources.' He laughed and looked around.

'We can't stay here,' she said and after taking her handbag she pushed him to go outside.

'You are not very hospitable.'

'I don't live alone, so it's better to be outside.'

'Okay. Do you want to go for a walk in the park?' he asked.

'Yes. I need a walk. What did you discover?'

'First, I want you to tell me why you didn't keep your promise?'

'What promise?' She was surprised.

'I was going to write your story.'

'I thought you got it. I saw your name under one of the articles.'

'I have my sources, but it was no thanks to you. So, why didn't you keep your promise?'

They walked slowly towards the park. Thea stopped and turned to Bobby. He seemed surprised by this.

'What's wrong?' he asked.

'I forgot ... I just forgot about you,' said Thea. 'I'm really sorry, but everything I had to go through, I just turned off.'

Thea sat down on the first bench she saw and covered her face with her hands. Bobby had helped her through a tough time and kept his promise not to tell anyone he saw her. However, she had not kept hers to him.

'Koev told me about the case,' Bobby told her and tried to remove her hands from her face and calm her down. 'But you, you took my question very seriously. I wouldn't have asked you if I knew you would be so upset.'

'Koev?'

'Yes. He contacted me the day after I left you at the police station, and he promised me the whole story if I kept quiet until the investigation was over.'

'Well, after all, I also promised you,' said Thea, 'but so many things happened since then and I simply forgot, Bobby.'

'I guess that Koev shortened his story a lot, but that's not what I'm here for. One of my colleagues has discovered Sonya. Koev told me about her but made me promise not to publish anything until they found her. Well, according to my sources, the building she lives is quite close, five blocks from here.'

'You're kidding.' Thea looked at him in disbelief.

'I'm not. I wanted you to come with me and identify her before I called Koev. I know you saw her once.'

'I will never forget her face.'

'Okay then, let's go to her house.'

'I hope it's her,' Thea whispered and got up from the bench.

Five blocks down, Bobby stopped at the corner of a house and looked up at the building across the street.

'It looks like a big house, but there are several flats inside. Sonya is on the second floor. I'll ring the doorbell, and if you want, go up to the third floor and try to see her from the stairs.'

'Okay,' Thea said, quickly crossing the street and entering the cool entrance of the building. It was quiet and peaceful inside; no noise could be heard from the apartments. Thea climbed the stairs to the third floor and stared at the door where Bobby was standing. He looked at her questioningly, and after she nodded, he rang the bell. After the third ring, a noise was heard from the apartment. Slow footsteps approached the door and a female voice asked who it was.

'I'm from the neighbouring building. I live in apartment 9, just like you, and I think they delivered your package to me by mistake.'

The door slowly opened, and in the doorway, stood a woman with long hair tied in a braid.

'I didn't order anything, so it's not likely to be for me,' she said.

Bobby handed her a package with a name and address written on it and after she denied it was hers, he apologized for the trouble, and she closed the door.

'Is this her?'

'No, Bobby, unfortunately it's not her.'

'Too bad,' he said with disappointment showing on his face. 'I really thought it was her; the description matches perfectly.'

'Yes, but it's not her. Sonya's voice is hoarse, and her face is rounder.'

Thea and Bobby left the building, each lost in thought.

'What will you do now?' he asked.

'I will go home and read a book.'

'Have you had dinner?'

'No.'

'Do you want to get a sandwich and go for a walk in the park?'

'On one condition – I don't want to talk about what happened to me.'

'Okay,' he agreed.

They stopped in front of a sandwich wagon, got food and drinks, and sat down on one of the benches near the lake in the park.

'I don't know exactly what happened to you in the last few months, but you look scared and like life has taken its toll,' he said while swallowing part of his sandwich.

'You don't look good either,' she replied.

There were dark circles under Bobby's eyes, his smile was dull, and he wasn't talking as much as usual.

'I am tired. I'm working on a few stories and haven't slept well in weeks.'

'Do they pay you well for this?'

'Yes, but it takes all my time, and sometimes I wonder if it's worth it,' he admitted.

'But journalism is what you wanted to do since I've known you. Do you remember how you used to come and interview us like we were all famous?'

'Yeah, it was fun,' he laughed. 'But the cases I work on are not funny. Most are so brutal, and I can hardly believe they even exist.'

'Like my case?' Thea asked.

'Yes, your case is a good example of brutality. How old are you now, Thea? Nineteen? I'm three years older than you, and just by coming into contact with these stories is causing me to feel like I am dying little by little. You are actually involved. I don't even want to think about how you survived. You don't seem to have changed. Yes, you look tired, but inside you are the same. What has happened to you has not broken you. I wonder how you managed to stay true to yourself.'

'I'm changed, Bobby; you just haven't noticed the difference.'

'No, Thea, you haven't changed. You're the same, a little scared, but still with that look, with that belief that everything will be all right.'

Thea looked at Bobby, and their eyes met. 'I believe that I will do everything possible to find my daughter,' she said. 'It keeps me up at night and gets me up early in the morning. But let's not talk about that anymore.'

Thea turned the conversation to their childhood memories. About school and the troubles that Bobby often made back then. An hour later, he walked her to her flat. That night, when she went to bed, Thea fell asleep with a smile on her face for the first time in a long time. She dreamed that she was floating in the clouds and the sun was shining on her face.

When she opened her eyes, she saw that it was late in the morning. Thea had slept for over ten hours and felt new and refreshed. She made herself some coffee and for the first time since moving into the apartment had a long conversation with her roommates. They, like her, were going through a difficult period in their lives, but none of them talked about it. Instead, the three stood in front of the television screen and chatted about trivial matters. At 3 p.m., Koev called her to check how she was and to tell her that he had scheduled another meeting with Georgi the next morning. This time, Thea was not bothered by the fact that she had to talk to him. On the contrary, what Bobby had said about sensing that she had not changed internally made her more confident in herself and in continuing to search for information about her daughter. She would do her best to find out where Maria was. Thea had to calmly face Georgi and challenge him to speak. Mary had taught her that and Thea would be grateful for that for the rest of her life.

Thea had a peaceful evening and fell asleep the moment she got into bed. The next morning, she felt even more rested. When Koev saw her, a small smile appeared on his face.

'You sent Bobby.' Thea immediately understood this after seeing his smug smile.

'Yes. I was worried about you and decided to send you a friend. Bobby keeps asking me about you, so I called him and told him where to find you.'

'And the story about Sonya? Was it made up?'

'What story?' Koev asked and was genuinely surprised.

'One of Bobby's sources had found a woman with Sonya's description, and Bobby and I went to see if it was her.'

'Was she?'

'No, but she looked a lot like her.'

'Where did you see her?'

'A few blocks from here.'

'You should have called me. Sonya has a sister who we are also looking for. You may have seen her.'

'Perhaps.'

'Tell me the address,' Koev said. After Thea dictated it to him, he started talking on the phone. Thea could hear him talking about the arrest.

'I'm sorry I didn't tell you. I didn't know Sonya had a sister.'

'Don't worry about it. Now focus on your conversation with Georgi.'

Thea nodded, and as she looked at the gloomy building, all the courage she had gathered over the past two days evaporated. As they passed from one corridor to another, Thea could hear her footsteps and those of the others beside her. They echoed, and with every approach to a cell, someone's eyes were fixed on them. The feeling of being watched by criminals was horrible. Her skin turned pale, and her eyes began to look scared. Koev noticed the difference in her mood and quickly led her back to the lobby of the building.

'You can't go in scared to see Georgi. You need to pull yourself together,' he said. He bought them both coffee from the vending machine and ushered her outside. 'I thought you were ready to talk to him, but apparently you are not.'

'I'm ready – give me five minutes to recover.'

'As long as it takes, Thea; you don't have to rush.'

Koev wanted to say something more, but his phone rang, and he walked away to speak, leaving her alone with her thoughts. Thea was sipping her warm coffee and trying to calm down. She remembered the birth; she remembered her escape from the hamlet and her return there. Everything she had gone through had seemed manageable then. Why couldn't she muster the strength now? She was angry with herself. Her kidnapping and the burning remains of the man in the furnace had made her more sensitive and weaker. Mary had told her that as the main witness, Thea would have to appear in court frequently and testify against Georgi and her family. She had told her that would be the hardest part because she would have to talk about them, and they would be watching her. Now, sitting here, Thea wondered if she was going to be able to handle it. She couldn't look Georgi in the eyes; how would she feel if it was a member of her family? It would be painful, but she had to do it. She continued to sip her coffee and stare at Koev's back. Hardly anyone else would be as responsive to her as he was. As though sensing her gaze, he turned and smiled at her, then ended the conversation he was having and sat down next to her.

'What's going on in your beautiful head? What are you thinking about?'

'I think we need to find another way to find these children. I'm scared of him, and he'll feel it the moment I walk into the cell. That will change everything; he won't treat me the same way anymore. I will be like all the other women.'

Koev patted her hand in understanding. 'Let's find another way to locate your daughter,' he said, helping her up.

'The other day, I wanted to talk with you about something,' he said while driving. 'I want to make you a consultant on this case. It will be difficult to convince my bosses, since you are a victim and a witness, but I think your desire to find Maria will be a great plus for us. What do you think about that?'

'If I become a consultant, can I look at all the documents in the investigation?'

'That's the idea. Now, I can't give you details about events and suspects, but if my bosses and you allow you to be part of my team, you will be able to look at all the information we have. There is something that has eluded me for years. My intuition is that I was on the wrong track with the first case. Listen, Thea, I haven't told anyone until now, but after asking everyone, after getting to know Georgi better, I have a feeling that something is wrong. I thought he was pulling the strings, that he was moving things, but now I don't think so anymore.'

'What do you mean? You saw the information on his laptop, all the phone calls, the addresses of the adoptive parents, as well as his contact with Sonya and her husband.'

'Trust me, Thea, something is not right. And I began to doubt the moment he started spending more time with you in the hamlet. There are times when transactions were made from his laptop, and he wasn't physically there. They were not done remotely. I think someone else is behind all this.'

'What? But who?'

'I don't know. That's why I want you to look at everything we found. You know more people in the area, and you know who he talked to. One of the people around him is the mastermind behind it all. It's not Georgi, it's not anyone from the hamlet, including your family. It has to be someone smart enough to link everyone in their network and have a good knowledge of disguising financial transactions and opening offshore accounts under false names.'

'But what made you doubt it?' Thea asked.

'My intuition told me that something was wrong, but I only realized it when we found you at the glass factory. If Georgi was in charge, he would know where Maria really is. He would also know that the other children were not where they should be. In my opinion, the person dealing with this started changing addresses at some point. He probably wanted to protect himself from Georgi's weakness, or if he found out that Georgi was the father of some of the sold children, he insured himself in case Georgi decided to look for them later. Whatever the reason, the last thirty-nine children have still not been found. The stories of the other kids are identical; the same people handed them over to their new parents. After that, something changed, and Georgi probably didn't know about the change.'

Thea listened to Koev and thought he was right. She had noticed that Georgi had a hard time with computers, and sometimes she or her brother Rado had helped him with one thing or another.

'And if he paid someone to do his bank accounts?'

'That doesn't explain why he didn't control where the kids went. Most likely he was getting his share and no longer cared. He does not match the profile; the person who created this network controls it. Georgi knows how to control people, to pressure them, but in my opinion, he is only a link in this case.'

'Did you check what books he was reading in detention?'

'Yes. Both are by the same author, Boris Monov. I have picked up copies to read.'

'Will you get copies for me too?'

'Yes, I will order them as soon as we go to the office.'

'I thought you were going to take me back to the apartment.'

'No, I want you to come with me, and I'll show you something. While you're there, I'll talk to my bosses. Are you willing to work with me?'

'Yes.'

'Well then. Don't tell anyone about our conversation.'

'Do you suspect any of your colleagues?' she asked in amazement.

'I suspect everyone except you,' Koev said and turned to look her straight in the eyes. Thea guessed that he already had a suspect, but he didn't tell her who it was. Koev needed her to tie things up, she thought, staring out the window. It was already summer, and Thea couldn't believe that she had given birth only a few months ago. So much had happened since then that she felt as if she had already lived a whole human life. The change in direction this morning felt like a cold shower to her. What else did she have to go through to find Maria? Couldn't fate just bring them together? Why did it have to be so complicated? And who was behind all this, she wondered.

Koev and Thea travelled to the office in silence. When they arrived, he sat her in his office and went to talk to some of his colleagues. Mary greeted her, and she waited for Koev, who took almost an hour.

'I want you to look at these pictures,' he told her and turned his computer so that she could also see what was on the monitor. The photos were taken in front of the church in Bolengrad, and they showed several people talking. Thea recognized Georgi and a man from the hamlet. She had not seen the other people. The last photo showed a woman standing in the back, but Thea recognized the shoes and bag, which were an unusual colour.

'This is Dr. Ivanova; she is a gynaecologist at the municipal hospital. But she doesn't seem to be talking to them, does she?'

'I don't know, Thea. The photos were taken after a celebration in the church. Everyone gets out of the church. How do you know the doctor?'

'My mother took me to her when I found out I was pregnant. She examined me and confirmed the pregnancy.'

'Did she ask you who the father was? Did she ask you a lot of questions?'

'Yes. Now that I think about it, when I told her that Georgi was the father, she laughed and said, "Of course it's Georgi". At the time, I didn't pay attention; I thought that she meant the name Georgi; you know it is common in the town. But now that you ask me, she probably had him in mind.'

'In our opinion, she informed on women who were pregnant by the wrong man,' Koev said thoughtfully. 'She's certainly part of the network. I'm going to call her in for questioning today. Are you sure it's her?'

'Yes, as I said, no one else wears shoes and a bag of this colour.'

Koev nodded and left the office again. This time he returned after about two hours, carrying two bags of food in his hands.

'Are you hungry?'

'Yes,' Thea said. He motioned for her to follow him, and they both ended up in one of the offices on the top floor of the building. Koev ate in silence, so deep in thought that Thea had the feeling that he did not realize that she was there. Whatever was going on in his head, it was nothing good because every now and then, all she heard was 'Hmm ...' and saw him shake his head in disbelief. Thea didn't recognise that part of his character. She had always felt his presence; now he seemed to be playing chess with himself and didn't want anyone watching his moves. Thea was standing off to the side, trying to eat as quietly as possible so as not to interrupt his thoughts. She was interested in watching him. Their lunch – if you could call it that – took about ten minutes. The sound of a door opening interrupted Koev's thoughts. He quickly ate the rest of his sandwich and then told Thea that they should return to his office.

Thea was left alone for an hour again. Koev had left the building, and his colleagues came from time to time to ask her if he had returned. She was sitting on the chair in the empty office and reading one of Boris Monov's books. She didn't like the story, but she kept reading, in order to understand why

Georgi was interested in these two books. She had read a quarter of the story when Koev returned and told her that his bosses had not agreed to her being a consultant on the case. Thea couldn't hide her disappointment. Koev was also not satisfied.

'Of course, my bosses are right. You are our key witness, and if you enter the investigation, the defence will challenge every statement you make.'

'But …' Thea was speechless.

'I'm sorry, Thea, they have forbidden you from coming here. From now on we will have to work independently.'

'What do you mean?'

'I hired a private investigator on your behalf. I hope you don't mind.'

'What? Who is he?'

'A very good friend of mine. You can work with him on your daughter's case, but what I want you to promise me is that as soon as you find any information that can help me, you will call me. Do we understand each other?'

'But why?'

'Don't ask me questions. Dimitar will explain everything to you tomorrow morning.'

Thea looked at him confused. Something had happened in the last few hours, but Koev couldn't tell her what.

'But I don't have money to pay him.'

'Do not worry about it. Now go home and rest. Dimitar will come to pick you up tomorrow morning at seven.'

'Okay,' she said and slowly started to leave the office.

'Thea, remember not to say anything to anyone about our conversation.'

'I will not say anything,' she promised and left.

'I hope you find her before we do.'

Thea started to go back into the office, but he closed the door in her face and motioned for her to leave. His behaviour puzzled her. Was someone threatening him or threatening her and her child? *What had happened today?* she wondered and unconsciously pressed the book she had been reading to her chest. Perhaps within its pages was the answer.

Thea went back to the apartment, greeted her roommates, and retired to her room to read Monov's book. At some point someone rang the doorbell; one of her roommates opened it and brought her a package.

'A courier brought this for you. He said to open it right away.'

Thea thanked her, and after waiting for her roommate to close the door, she turned her attention to the package. It had only *Thea* written on it, and the handwriting was Koev's. She found a pair of scissors and opened the package. Inside were some photos and Boris Monov's second book. Thea looked at the pictures but didn't recognize any of them. All of the photos were taken on one of the streets in Bolengrad. They were of people walking down the street, and Thea didn't know exactly who the target of the photo was. There were men, women, and children on the street. People were sitting in front of one of the cafes. It was impossible for Thea to say why Koev had sent her these pictures, but if he had, then there was something important about them. She looked at the photos once more, then looked at the book he had sent her and saw a note sticking out of one of the pages. After reading the writing, Thea gasped. 'From here on you are ALONE', Koev had written. The message was clear; Thea was not to call him and trust no one. But why? What had happened today? She lay down on the bed and stared at the ceiling. What other surprises awaited her, she wondered. Then she got up and put the books and pictures in her handbag. Just then, her phone rang.

'Thea, how are you?' Mary asked.

'Okay. And you?'

'I'm fine. Koev came out and my boss asked me to call you and tell you that you have to vacate the apartment within two weeks.'

Thea opened her mouth to say something, but she didn't know what.

'Georgi and everyone involved in your case are in prison, and the head of the Regional Police Department he doesn't think you're in danger anymore and took you off the protected witness list. My colleagues recommend that you don't leave the country until the trial is over.'

Thea still couldn't make sense of what she heard. The management refused to protect her. But why? Everyone knew about the connections Georgi had in the outside world. And where did they expect her to go?

'Thea? Thea, can you hear me?'

'Yes. I understand, within two weeks I have to vacate the room. Can I keep the job, or should I look for a new one?'

'Sorry, Thea, you should look for another job. This is just a cover, I hope you understand,' Mary said, a sympathetic note creeping into her voice.

'Where is Koev?'

'I don't know. He left his office this afternoon and said he would come back tomorrow at noon. He said it was personal and unrelated to work. Do you want me to tell him to call you tomorrow when he gets back?'

'No, I'll call him later. Thanks, Mary.'

'Call me if you need anything.'

'I will. Thanks!' said Thea and ended the conversation. They had given her two weeks to move out and had sent her away without money, a job, or a place to stay. Koev was right; from now on she was alone. She sat wearily on the bed and thought about where she could go, where she could work, and who she could ever trust. A face popped into her mind –Bobby. The other person she firmly trusted was unlikely to help her, and she lived outside the capital. Mrs. Mariola was probably still very disappointed in her. Thea still remembered her look when she saw her and Georgi in that restaurant. *What had she thought then?* Thea wondered. *Probably nothing good.* Thea wrapped herself in the thick blanket and thought back to those days when Mrs. Mariola had patronized her. The teacher had probably then visited her mother and offered her money. It was also an attempt at buying and selling, Thea thought. Why did she get involved with Georgi? *Why did you make your life so complicated?* she reproached herself. Then she thought of Maria, and the tears unconsciously began to flow. The word *ALONE* written by Koev had pierced her heart. Thea had grown up in a large family; she was never alone, and now she had to learn to live with her loneliness. Her thoughts were intertwining with each other, her tears were flowing like a river, and Thea didn't know how to stop this feeling of helplessness. Where to go? What to do? How to find Maria? How will she stand up to her family and testify against them? All these feelings kept her up late at night.

The next day, the ringing of her phone woke her up. When she looked at the dial, she saw that it was ten minutes past seven in the morning. The phone number that was calling her urgently was unfamiliar to her, but Thea decided to pick up.

'It's been a long time since seven,' said an unknown voice.

'Who is calling?' she asked.

'Dimitar, the private detective. We were supposed to meet at 7 a.m., don't you remember?'

'I remember now. Sorry, I'll be with you in five minutes.'

'Okay. I'll wait for you in the car.'

Thea got up quickly, straightened up, and ran out the door. When he saw her leaving, a man waved at her and invited her to get into the car. Then he handed her a cup of coffee.

'Koev assumed that you would have had a hard evening and asked me to bring you coffee.'

'Very nice of him.'

'Very nice? No, *unusual* is the word. He's never asked me for a favour before, and I daresay I'm his best friend. Your case has thrown him off the rails.'

'I guess it has.'

'What happened yesterday?' Dimitar asked.

'I don't know. I was in his office, then he sent me away, saying that you would help me find my daughter. Then his colleague called me that I have two weeks to move out of the room and find a new job.'

'You are kidding?'

'I'm not. This reminds me that I have to go to work in two hours. I didn't go yesterday, and I have to explain why.'

'But why did they remove you from the protected witness list?' Dimitar wondered.

'I have no idea. I don't know what happened yesterday, but it was like the world came crashing down on me.'

Dimitar looked ahead, then started the engine and drove north. Thea took occasional sips of her coffee and wondered where they were going and whether she should trust him.

'Calm down, I won't kidnap you. We are going to my office to talk there in peace. In the meantime, I'll try to contact Koev and find out what's going on.'

'His colleague Mary called me last night and told me that he was away on personal business and would be back sometime today.'

'Personal matters? Koev? His personal life is me when we go to the pub for a few beers. Koev has no personal life.'

'There may be someone new in his life that you don't know about.'

'You were the new person in his life. Koev only thinks about your case, how to find your daughter and the other children.'

Thea said nothing, and Dimitar continued to drive in silence as well. When they arrived, Thea was surprised at the sight of the building they entered. As they walked to his office, several people passed him and greeted him.

'Good morning, boss.'

'Hi, Markov.'

'How are you, boss?'

'I'm fine, Pavlov.'

Thea realized that Dimitar wasn't just some private detective; he was the head of a major detective agency. She looked around, and everywhere she saw modern equipment and young, dynamic people crossing the corridors.

'You are impressed.' He smiled.

'That's right. I was expecting a small office on the outskirts.'

'Koev and I studied together. He was the best, and he accepted a job in the government organization, and I headed for the private sector. I'd say we're both good at this job.'

'Koev said he hired you.'

'Actually, that's partly why we're here. He paid for you to hire me, but it's really a favour between friends. I will enter into a contract with you for a minimum fee, and I will work for you as I work with my wealthier clients.'

'Oh, I didn't know that was your arrangement. When I start work, I can pay you.'

'Don't worry about the financial part of the matter. It is only fictitious. The important thing is that we help you with our resources to find your daughter and the other children.'

'Okay.' Thea calmed down and sat down in the chair that Dimitar pointed out to her.

'Now, I know we don't have much time, so tell me everything from the very beginning.'

Thea began to tell him all she could remember, and Dimitar recorded the conversation. As he listened, like any old man in his trade, he took notes in a large notebook. He asked her questions and encouraged her to share what she felt and what she thought about everything that had happened to her. At ten minutes to ten he ended the conversation and asked someone to drive her to the factory where she worked and to bring her back in the evening.

Thea went to the factory, but to her surprise, she was not allowed inside. She was no longer on the list of workers. She was told that her salary would be deposited into the bank account, and with that, the supervisor sent her away.

'Don't worry, we will find you a job.' Dimitar tried to calm her down, and he asked the driver to take her back to the office. Thea spent the whole day there trying to tell everything she knew about her case.

'Okay,' said Dimitar, 'let's find you a free desk. I want you to look at photos and materials of children who have disappeared over the years and tell me if you recognize the children or the parents.'

Thea spent a few more hours at Dimitar's agency. Finally, she got tired and asked him to take her to her apartment. Before leaving, Dimitar promised to call her when he had news. Thea was once again alone with her thoughts and worries. She had to find a job and a place to live tomorrow morning. She opened Boris Monov's book again and tried to concentrate on reading. For some reason, however, what was written in the note by Koev kept appearing in front of her eyes. 'ALONE'. Thea wondered if there wasn't more to it than she'd let on. What had Koev tried to tell her, she wondered. And what the hell had changed yesterday? Why had Koev sent her away so quickly? Something had happened that day, something that changed her fate, and from a protected and important witness to the investigation, she had been put on the unnecessary witness list. She should have contacted Koev, but this note seemed to warn her not to do so. Thea tossed and turned in bed for a long time and fell asleep only in the early hours.

When she woke up, she looked at the phone's display and saw the message 'No SIM card found'. After taking the card out and putting it back in the phone, Thea realized that Regional Police Department had blocked her calls. It was only a matter of time before she was kicked out of the flat. The shock of what was happening took its toll on her, and little by little, Thea allowed panic to overwhelm her. She had no money, nowhere to go, and all her contacts were deleted. Her life collapsed in an instant. Thea looked out the window and saw a crowd of passers-by hurrying to cross the street. Everyone had somewhere to go, in some direction, as she stood in the little room bemoaning her fate. Then she remembered what she had been through and how, just like that day, she thought that somewhere there was someone who could help her, someone she could trust.

'Bobby,' she whispered and remembered that Koev had sent him to her. It was as if he had been preparing her for this. Thea packed as much luggage as she had into one bag and left the flat. She didn't want to go back to that room again, but if she couldn't find Bobby, or if he wasn't willing to help her, she would have to go back. Thea put the key in her purse and headed to the editorial office of the newspaper where the journalist worked. He had told her where he worked the day, he came to visit her. As she crossed the street, Thea unconsciously headed for the block where the woman who looked like Sonya lived. Something made her want to go back there again and talk to her. When she stood at the door of her flat, Thea hesitated and started to leave. At that moment, the door opened, and the woman invited her in.

'For several years I have had pains in my legs and cannot go outside, and my only entertainment is watching who enters and who leaves the block. I saw you the other day with that young man who was talking to me about a shipment. Why had you actually come then?' asked the woman as she placed sweets and a glass of water on the small table in front of Thea.

'You look a lot like a woman I used to know.'

'I assume you are talking about my sister Sonya. Many people come to ask me about her these days, and they all say they are her friends. Were you friends?'

'No, actually she is the person I last saw with my daughter.'

'I understand,' said the woman. 'Sorry to hear that. By the way, my name is Tanya, and I am the older sister. Sonya always got into trouble, and when she met her husband, it seemed that trouble began to find her even more. For years I tried to help her, but I finally gave up and cut ties with her.'

'How long since you saw her?'

'I told the others that I haven't seen her for ten years, but the truth is that five years ago, she came home with a child. Someone had chased her, and I believed her story, as she was bruised all over. She told me that someone tried to kill the baby and she managed to save it. I sheltered her for two days and took the child anonymously to one of the nearby hospitals. I said I found it in front of the block. Soon after, Sonya left without saying goodbye. Was this child yours? You're young; it was hardly yours.'

'No. I gave birth on March ninth, and the same day, your sister and her husband came and took my daughter. I've been looking for her ever since.'

'As far as I understood from a gentleman who visited me recently, my sister is wanted by the police.'

'Do you have any idea where she went?'

'No. I'd love to help you, but I haven't spoken to her since that day.'

'It's a pity. She is the only person who knows where my daughter is,' said Thea and got up from the chair. 'Is there a place she'd go where you've both been? Your parents' house or someone you know from childhood?'

Tanya thought, then got up and walked slowly out of the room. She came back with some pictures.

'This is our villa in Greece. Our father was Greek, and after the divorce with my mother, Sonya and I often went there. We are all his children's heirs, four in all. Might be a good idea to check there. The city is called Kavala, and it is on the seashore. It is very nice town with friendly people.'

'Do you remember the address of the villa?' Thea asked.

'No, but you can take this picture and show it to the people there.'

'Thanks!'

'I hope you find your daughter. I lost mine when I was twenty-nine years old. She died of cancer. I know what it's like to mourn your child.'

'Thank you very much!' said Thea again and hugged the old woman. Then, with the photo in her trembling hand, she left the flat. For the first time, there was a concrete lead, and although Tanya wasn't sure Sonya was there, Thea felt excited that she might be able to find her.

Leaving the building, reality hit her again. She was without money, and soon without a roof over her head. The only idea that came to her mind again was to ask Bobby for help. Thea did not know the streets of Sofia very well; from the beginning of her stay, she had been guided or given rides. When she stood on the road, she wondered which way to go. Finally, she asked a random person, who directed her how to get to Bobby's office by public transport.

'What normal person would want to walk all the way there?' He had sounded surprised. Now she could keep track of where the bus was going, and she would eventually get there. It took her three hours to walk to the centre of Sofia and another hour to find the office of the newspaper Bobby worked for. When she mentioned his name, no one asked her who she was. She was just led to his desk, where he was typing something on the computer with his head down.

'Bobby, this woman wants to talk to you,' said the man and left.

'Thea, what are you doing here?' Bobby asked, surprised to see her.

'Can we talk somewhere else?'

'Of course. Come on.'

Thea followed him to a small garden outside the building. It had started to drizzle, and Bobby changed direction and took her to sit under a canopy in a café.

'Do you want me to get you something to drink?'

'No, but I wouldn't refuse food,' admitted Thea.

Bobby got in line and looked at her as he waited. When he returned with food and drink, he had her sit at one of the tables and allowed her to eat in peace.

'Why are you here? Why aren't you at work?' he asked.

'The Regional Police Department removed me from the list of important witnesses; they left me without a job and a phone, and I only have a few days to find a place to live.'

Thea recited all this so quickly that she was startled by the outpouring of words.

'But why?'

'I don't know. Something happened that day in the office, and Koev sent me away without explaining what. Then Mary called to tell me I was no longer on their witness list.'

'Who is Mary, and what did Koev say?'

'Mary is his colleague, and Koev had taken a few hours for personal matters.'

Bobby was watching Thea, and the surprise on his face was clear.

'They kicked you out with no money, no phone and no job and put you in danger. Georgi can find you, even from the prison.'

'I know. And I know it's not ideal to bring you into this, but you're the only person I trust. I came to you because I need help. I need to get to Kavala, Greece, as quickly as possible.'

'Greece? But why all the way there? What is there?'

'Sonya might be there.'

'Are you sure?'

'No, but I have to check. Only she knows where my daughter is, and her sister said they had a villa there.'

'Her sister?'

'Yes, the woman you spoke to a few days ago. I spoke to her a few hours ago.'

Bobby opened his mouth to say something, but then stopped. 'Is that all your luggage?' he asked.

'Yes.'

'You can stay with me if you want.'

'That would be very kind, but I must go to Greece as soon as possible.'

'Do you have money?'

'No. I told you I have no money, no phone. I have nothing.'

'Okay, here's what we're going to do. I will go and buy you a ticket to Kavala. Nowadays many people travel there. I'll give you money, but it won't be much, because I'm about to get paid, and I'm not very thrifty, to be honest. We will also get you a SIM card. Do you need anything else?'

'No.'

'I wish I could come with you, but I'm in the middle of something, and I won't be able to.'

'Don't worry.'

'When you get back, however, promise me that the story will be mine. And this time, promise not to forget to tell me about it.'

'I won't forget.' Thea smiled and sighed in relief.

Bobby went back to his office and managed to buy a ticket for the next day.

'In the summer, many people travel there for a few days,' he told her.

Buying a SIM card was also quick. Bobby gave his details and entered the most important phone numbers into her contact list.

'You can call me anytime, but if I'm interviewing someone, I won't be able to answer you. You'll have to wait for me to call you back. If you manage to find Sonya, send me a message with her name and I will call you as soon as I see it. If you're in trouble, call me until I answer.'

'Thanks, Bobby! I will give you all the money back as soon as I can.'

'Don't worry about it. Give me your story, and we're done.'

'Okay,' Thea promised.

Bobby drove her to the flat where he lived and went back to work. There were four men living in his flat, but two were out of the country and the other was working late, so there would be no one to bother her. Thea left her luggage in his room and sat down on the sofa. His library was full of books, a TV was installed in the middle of the wall, and in the other corner was a large computer monitor that Bobby probably worked on when he was at home. His room was very well arranged, as if it followed an order, something Thea hadn't seen before. Even in Mrs. Mariola's house there were objects out of place. Thea thought that maybe Bobby used a cleaner, but after seeing the two locks on the door, she decided that he was unlikely to let anyone in there to touch his things. All the folders on his desk were meticulously numbered and arranged.

Thea stepped forward and stared at the folders in front of her. She didn't expect to see her name, but it was there. When she opened the folder, there was almost nothing inside. There was only her picture from the school album and brief information about her: her name, her daughter's name, and Georgi's name. Thea wondered why he only wrote that. Bobby certainly knew a lot more about her case. She looked at the picture once more, gently caressed the face there that didn't seem to be hers. Then she closed the folder and sat down on the sofa. She couldn't wait to go to Greece and find the villa where Sonya could be. Bobby had promised to take her to the bus station where the bus left early in the morning.

Thea thought about her family. What was everyone doing now? Were they in the same cell together, or had they been separated? Bad or good, they were her family, and she missed them all very much now. Kinship is a strange thing, she thought. Just because they were her family, she was willing to forgive them. But Georgi, Maria's father, she could not forgive. *What kind of father sells his own child?* she had asked herself many times. There was a simple answer – a psychopath. Only a person with deep mental problems could do this. And Sonya, why did she choose to help people like him? She was a woman; she should understand a mother's pain. Was she forced by circumstances or was it of her own accord? It reminded Thea of the child Sonya had taken to her sister. Thea didn't ask Tanya if it was a boy or a girl, but if she called Koev to go and question her again, maybe she would give him more information.

Thea started to call the lieutenant, but the note written by him appeared again in front of her eyes, and that stopped her. She would ask Bobby to send him her new phone number and ask Koev to call her when he could. Thea looked around Bobby's room again and looked at the books on his shelf. She wondered if she should take a book and read; then she remembered that she already had one, took it out of her bag, and read. No matter how hard she tried to understand the meaning of what was written on the pages, she couldn't. The book had too many unrelated characters. Thea kept losing the thread and finally gave up reading. Tired from the tension of the past few days, she fell asleep, hugging a small pillow and putting the book aside.

At eleven o'clock at night, Bobby came back and woke her up.

'Did you manage to sleep?' he asked.

'Yes.'

'I brought dinner. If you want, let's eat,' he said and went to the kitchen.

Thea followed him, found utensils, and placed them on the table. Bobby pulled out takeaway cartons and sat down, and she sat across from him.

'A hard day?' Thea asked.

'One of the hardest.' He sighed.

'What happened?'

'Mass suicide in an abandoned building. I'm definitely going to have nightmares tonight.'

'How many people died?'

'Twelve. There are also two survivors who are still in a coma.'

'Why would anyone want to end their life?' Thea was surprised.

'Because they see no point in continuing. Maybe they don't have one.'

Thea felt the depression come over him. What he had heard and seen had visibly shocked him.

'Promise me something, Thea.'

'What?'

'Promise me you'll find your daughter.'

'I promised myself, I don't see why I shouldn't promise you too. We don't even need to discuss it.'

'I need a happy ending story, you know? Otherwise, I'll go crazy soon.'

'Why don't you change your job, Bobby? You don't seem happy to me; you haven't been the same since you worked for this newspaper.'

'I can't. That's my nature – I like to deal with news.'

'Then change the crime news to sports news,' suggested Thea.

'You think that in sports the news is always good? The last time I wrote a story in the sports column, it was about a lifelong athlete who, in a silly accident, developed an eye tic that prevented him from concentrating. His whole life collapsed in an instant. There are sad stories everywhere, Thea, but of all the ones I've heard so far, yours is the saddest.'

'But it will have a happy ending,' Thea said, and she really believed it. She and Maria would be together someday.

After they had eaten, Bobby continued to work, and Thea drifted off into sleep again. This time she had no nightmares, and her sleep was peaceful. Bobby woke her up at three in the morning and the two sleepily drove to the bus station.

Kavala was not far from Sofia, and Thea expected to arrive there in just a few hours. She said goodbye to Bobby, put what little luggage she had in the luggage compartment, and settled into the window seat. To her surprise, the bus was full of passengers. Most of the passengers were tourists who had decided to visit Greece for a few days; the others seemed to be Bulgarians working or living in Greece who had visited Bulgaria to see their relatives. Thea saw that despite the early hour, there were smiles on most of the passengers' faces. How she wished she could smile too. Maybe on the bus ride back she would, maybe she would find Maria and come back with her. Thea allowed herself to daydream as they travelled south. Then she drifted off, and when she awoke, she saw that a sixty-year-old woman had taken up residence next to her. The woman was large and the type of person who kept talking, often asking questions and not waiting to hear the answers. When the woman saw that Thea was awake, she turned to her with a big smile.

'Did you wake up, sweetheart? Oh, sorry, I probably pushed you unintentionally, but those seats are so uncomfortable. I'm Elizabeth, by the way. What's your name, honey? Teodora? How could your mother call you that? It's an old name, isn't it?'

'My name is Teodora too,' shouted a woman. 'There is nothing wrong with the name.'

'Well, now, madam, I didn't mean to offend you. So. why are you alone, Teodora? A young girl like you should have a boyfriend to take her on vacations. When I was young, I never travelled alone.'

Elizabeth was talking loudly, and everyone on the bus was listening. After a while, there wasn't a passenger who didn't know her story. Often her stories were so funny that everyone on the bus laughed heartily. Thea listened and looked at the woman in rapture. She had never met someone like her before. Although she was chubby, Elizabeth looked good for her age. She was wearing a colourful patterned dress, and her makeup and earrings matched.

'She's artistic,' said the woman from the seat behind Thea. 'I haven't laughed like that in years.'

'Well, my life is like that, dynamic.' Elizabeth turned to her. 'I outlived three men. And to the last one I said, laugh, laugh, life is good, and he became more and more miserable with each passing day. He only watched TV; he never liked to enjoy life. And you darling, why don't you smile?' she asked Thea.

'I wish I could,' Thea said quietly.

'Of course, you can. You are young, you are beautiful, you will get married one day, you will have children. Here, you see, this will be your life. Drink of it while you can and while you are young.'

'Not everyone's life goes that way,' said the woman in the back seat, who had seen Thea's worry.

'Well, there are exceptions,' Elizabeth said and briefly looked at Thea. Then she continued to tell stories from her life, but Thea was no longer amused. What Elizabeth had said made her think. She hadn't thought of herself as an 'exception' until now, but she realized that stories like hers were rare. If she tried to tell anyone about her life, they would hardly believe her. Thea sighed. Until recently, living in the hamlet made her different; now if her story came out, she would be seen as an exception, and all she wanted was to be accepted as normal. She wanted her life to be like everyone else's, as Elizabeth had just described it.

'How long will you stay in Kavala?' asked the woman behind her.

'I don't know.'

'Who will you stay with?'

'I will rent a hotel room when I arrive.'

'You can come and visit me if you want. I broke up with my husband a few months ago, and now I live alone.'

Thea was surprised at the invitation. At first, she decided to refuse, then she thought it would be good to know someone local.

'Okay, I'll check in at the hotel, and then I'll go out for a walk.'

'I can take you around and show you the city. I'm off today and tomorrow.'

'I will be very thankful. I don't know anyone in Kavala.'

'Don't worry, there is a large Bulgarian community, and if you need help, everyone will respond.'

'Great,' said Thea and thought that maybe she would find Sonya's villa quickly.

Thea was no longer listening to Elizabeth's stories, but stared out of the window, waiting for them to cross the border. No one in her family had ever left the country before, and it was a great experience for her. When Thea was little, she often dreamed of traveling to other countries, and Greece was the first place she wanted to visit. Once they entered Greek territory, Thea smiled. Maybe Maria was there. Maybe she would find her and get her back. This was her new dream. Whether it was doable, time would tell.

When they arrived in Kavala, Thea became worried. Seeing her worry, the woman in the back seat stood next to her and offered to help her find a hotel.

'My name is Rayna,' she introduced herself. 'And you, as everyone on the bus found out, are Teodora, right?'

'Actually, everyone calls me Thea.'

'Okay, Thea, let's find you a hotel.'

After only half an hour, Thea was settled in a beautiful hotel room with a view of the sea. It was a nice sunny day with a slight breeze, and Thea stared out the window for a few minutes. She had agreed to meet Rayna in an hour. She took the picture of the villa Tanya had given her and went down to the lobby to ask about the house. However, none of the staff knew which part of town the villa was located in. Thea decided to ask around in the cafes she saw on the street, and despite not knowing the language, she managed to explain what she was looking for. At the third café, a waiter confirmed that he knew where the villa was. When Rayna came, Thea asked her to translate the conversation between her and the waiter.

'He says the villa is not far. It's a little further up, but he doesn't know the owners.'

'Can he guide us?'

'Yes,' said Rayna. 'I'll take you there. Who lives in this villa?'

'An acquaintance of mine lived there years ago. She came with her sister and her father.'

'What is your acquaintance's name?'

'Tanya, and her sister's name is Sonya.'

'Tanya and Sonya? I don't know them, but I've lived here for fifteen years only. If they came before that, there is no way we would have met. Come, now we'll see who lives there.'

Thea and Rayna headed in the direction the waiter had shown them. When they arrived, Thea saw children's toys in the garden and her heart began to pound.

'Do you want us to call and ask about your acquaintance?'

'No, I don't want to bother them,' Thea said and quickly turned back. She would come later and watch who was in the house. However, her heart told her that Maria was there.

After a long walk and dinner with Rayna, Thea went back to the hotel for a while, and when she saw that it was almost dark, she started to walk to the villa. There were still many people on the streets, but when she arrived in front of the villa, it was deserted. The house itself was bright, and Thea could hear children's voices. Just as she decided to open the door and go inside, she felt someone standing next to her.

'What are you doing here?' Koev pulled her by the elbow and forced her to take a step back. Thea let out a small cry of surprise, then pulled her hand away and tried to free herself from him.

'I'm sure Maria is here,' she said while massaging the pain in her elbow.

'I think so too. How did you know she was here?'

'Tanya, Sonya's sister, told me about this villa. They came here often as children. And how did you find out?'

'There were council taxes paid and I tracked the payments. Thea, what were you planning to do? You weren't going to go inside, were you?'

'I want to see if Maria is there.'

'She is there – I saw her this morning.'

'She's not the only one in there, is she?' Thea asked. She had heard children's voices, songs, and the usual children's screams at play. There were at least two other children inside.

'A total of four children are inside. We can't go in, though, because I don't have jurisdiction here. I contacted my Greek colleagues. By tomorrow morning, they should arrive and check who is in the villa. Until then, you and I will have to wait.'

'I can't wait,' Thea said. Her eyes looked longingly at the window from which the children's voices could be heard. 'I want to see her now. I haven't seen her since she was born.'

'You can't go inside, Thea. The villa is private property, and you might be arrested. How are you going to get her back then? Think about it – it's risky, don't you understand?'

Thea continued to look at the villa, and Koev, worried that she would go inside, grabbed her elbow again. This time she didn't resist, and after a moment's hesitation, she signalled that she understood. He nudged her down the street, and she reluctantly strode to his side.

'Everything will be fine.' He tried to calm her down. 'Now that we know where she is, everything will be fine.'

They were just passing the fence of the villa when a woman came out into the garden with a baby in her arms. The woman was Sonya, and Thea had no doubt that the baby was Maria. She didn't need anyone to tell her it was her; her motherly instinct rose within her. The baby was crying, and Sonya was trying to calm her down by talking to her. Thea quickly turned back and had almost reached the gate when Koev's hand yanked her back sharply.

'What are you doing, Thea? You're going to ruin everything,' he whispered in her ear.

'I have to see her.' She tried to free herself, but Koev caught her and pressed her against the gate. Sonya approached with the baby, looked at them and, after seeing that Koev had leaned over Thea with the intention of kissing her, stepped back. When they heard the door of the house close, they both breathed a sigh of relief.

'It was close,' said Koev and pushed Thea, indicating that they should go. She walked beside him in a trance. She was so close to her daughter that she could almost touch her. And now with every step, she was moving farther away.

Koev accompanied her to her hotel room and stayed with her until morning. Thea could almost hear his thoughts; he didn't trust her, and she understood his concern. She hardly trusted herself; every fifteen minutes, she wondered if she should return and take her daughter from Sonya's arms. Then she would give up on the idea, letting herself dream of seeing her again in the morning and this time being able to hug her.

However, when Koev's Greek colleagues returned to the villa in the morning, there was no sign of Sonya and the kids. The woman had hurriedly packed what she could and left town.

For the first time since giving birth, Thea truly despaired. The feeling that she had lost track of her daughter forever took over her, entered her heart, and flowed in her veins. It was as if poison had been injected into her blood. Devastated, Thea travelled in the car with Koev, almost deranged with grief, praying, and crying continuously.

'We will find her,' he tried to reassure her, but his words seemed to be scattered in the space around them and did not reach her. Her eyes looked ahead and the pain in them was palpable, and her lips never stopped quivering as she uttered a silent prayer. *Why is all this happening? What did I do wrong?*

Koev sometimes caught these questions while driving to the capital. Thea spoke, but the voice was not hers, and when her tears stopped, the eyes were not hers. Koev had seen such eyes before. They were the eyes of a drowned man, of a man left without faith and home.

When they arrived, he put her up with Mary and asked her to take care of Thea. Mary, like him, was shocked by the change in Thea.

'What are we going to do?' she asked.

'I asked a friend to come and talk to her. He'll probably be here within an hour. If he can't calm her down, we'll have to take her to the hospital.'

They both looked over at Thea, who was curled up in bed. The young woman had taken a pillow and pressed it to her chest as if she was holding a child.

'Maybe it's better to take her to the doctor right away,' suggested Mary.

'Maybe, but I think Bobby will do better than the doctor. She has a lot of trust in him,' said Koev and left the two women in the house, engulfed by Thea's despair.

An hour later, Bobby arrived and tried to talk to Thea. However, she had closed herself in her imaginary world.

'I think she's in shock,' he said after almost two hours of trying to get her to relax. 'I'm not surprised after everything she's been through.'

'What are we going to do?' Mary asked.

'Let's give her some time to recover.'

'I'm worried about her.'

'Me too, but I know her well and I think if we take her to hospital, it will depress her even more. Let's let her sleep.'

'Koev said she hasn't slept since you took her to the bus station. Hope you are right and after she rests, she will get better.'

'If she continues to talk to herself in the morning, I will personally take her to hospital. However, if she is diagnosed as a life-threatening person, she will never be able to get her daughter back. I've read about several similar cases, and I don't want to take any chances. Koev did well to bring her here.'

'I hope you're right, Bobby,' Mary whispered and looked worriedly at the young woman, who continued to mutter to herself.

Thea was tired but trying to stay awake. She felt that something had broken inside her. She heard Bobby's words and felt Mary's sympathetic hugs, but it was as if their actions were through a barrier, an invisible wall that surrounded her body. She prayed to find her daughter again and searched for answers to the questions she asked herself, but finally the weariness in her body took over, and she fell asleep. Tears fell from her eyes as she slept. Mary came from time to time and wiped them away with a napkin that smelled of mint, and Thea sometimes inhaled deeply of that fresh scent. After a while, her tears stopped, her breathing evened out, and her hands relaxed, releasing the small pillow.

Thea slept soundly for almost ten hours. When she awoke, she heard muffled voices from the next room. She looked around and saw pictures of Mary and her family and calmed down. She was in a safe place. She slowly got up and walked to the door. When she opened it, three pairs of eyes stared at her. Mary, Bobby, and Koev were sitting at the small kitchen table. Before them were empty plates and glasses. All three were studying her, as if they were waiting for her to do or say something.

'Good morning,' she finally said.

'Actually, it's evening.' Koev smiled and got up to help her sit on the chair next to him. 'How do you feel?'

'Dizzy,' she admitted, holding her head in her hands. 'I have a headache.'

'You haven't eaten or drunk anything for two days,' Mary said and pushed a bottle of mineral water towards her. Then she got up and opened the fridge. 'I'll make you a sandwich.'

'Okay,' said Thea and looked at Koev.

'We are still looking for her,' he said and patted her hand sympathetically. 'We have a lead, but I don't want to get your hopes up.'

Thea nodded, took a sip of her water, and began to silently eat the sandwich Mary made her. While she was eating, she could feel the testing looks of the others.

'Why are you looking at me like that?' Thea finally asked, annoyed by their behaviour.

'When Koev brought you here, you weren't quite yourself. I guess we're all wondering if you're okay,' Bobby explained, looking her straight in the eyes.

'I am fine. Even my headache went away.'

'Hmm,' said Koev, continuing to observe her.

Thea ate, took another sip of water, and leaned back comfortably in the chair. Actually, she wasn't feeling well, but she was trying to hide her weakness from them. Her hands were shaking slightly, her skin was pale, and she felt dizzy. Thea avoided eye contact with Koev and Bobby. Instead, she picked up the water bottle and began to slowly rotate it between her palms, directing her gaze there.

'Why did you send me that note?' she asked Koev.

'To let you know that you can't trust anyone.'

'Even Mary?' Thea asked as she tried to mask a new pain in her stomach.

'I was transferred to work on another case.'

'Why? What changed?'

'In my opinion, one of my colleagues is involved in the child trafficking. Someone made a report saying that we were giving you too much importance in this case, and in just a few hours, our bosses had a change of heart. As you know, you are no longer on the witness list. Someone tried to kick you out of the game, but we don't know who yet.'

'The books that Georgi was reading –' Thea said quietly and moved her hands away from the bottle. The pain in her stomach was getting worse.

'What about them? I have never read a more boring book,' said Bobby.

'Exactly. They are boring and full of names.'

'Like in a police report,' Koev said and instantly understood what Thea wanted to say. She nodded, then hurried to the bathroom, bent over the toilet seat, and began to throw up.

Koev, Bobby, and Mary followed her. Mary helped her by holding her and running the water from the cistern every now and then.

'Everything will be fine,' she reassured her. 'This is a normal reaction of the body after a great stress. You'll feel better soon.'

'Now I am sure that you will be fine,' said Koev. His phone had been ringing for a few minutes, and he went to the kitchen to take the call. When he returned to the bathroom, a small smile appeared on his face. 'They found Sonya and the kids,' he said. 'They are in Greece.'

Thea looked over her shoulder at him and Koev saw the glint in her eyes.

'You can't come with me.'

'Stop me!' Thea said while washing her face with warm water.

'I will bring you some clothes to change into,' Mary said and left the bathroom.

'I will come to the border with Thea,' suggested Bobby.

'I thought you had work today,' Koev said, trying to prevent him coming along. 'You said you were working on some case.'

'Exactly,' Bobby said, and left the bathroom as well.

'If you come, you should not approach her.' Koev turned to Thea.

'Who? Sonya?'

'Sonya and your daughter.'

'I promise not to approach her. I won't do anything to jeopardize your career.'

'It's not about me, it's about you, and the sooner you realize it, the better. To get Maria back, you'll have to go to court. If you break any law, your chances are reduced. Do you understand the risk, Thea?'

Koev had raised his voice, and Thea shuddered at the echo in the bathroom.

'I understand,' she tried to assure him, but he seemed to feel her hesitation. 'Why do I have to go through court to get her back?'

'Because your case is different from the case of all the other sold children. We'll talk about that later. I don't have time now, and I have to go.'

She tried to stop him, but he grabbed her shoulders and shook her slightly, looking into her eyes.

'Thea, promise me you won't do anything wrong if you follow me with Bobby. Look at me!'

She was trying to avoid his gaze.

'Look at me! Any interference on your part could be fatal and you may never get custody of Maria.'

This time she looked into his eyes and nodded. Koev released her and she noticed that his hands were shaking.

'Okay, I'm going now. I'll text Bobby where to find me. Meanwhile, Mary will send you a list of everyone working in the department. As you travel, you can compare this list with the names in the books Georgi is reading.'

'I'll take care of it,' called Mary as she came in with clean clothes for Thea.

13

An hour later, Thea and Bobby were on their way to the Bulgarian-Greek border. The place where they were supposed to meet Koev was in an uninhabited area. Bobby had given Thea the list and the book, and she had been comparing names as they drove, saying the names out loud before crossing them off.

'Next on the list is Peev. I don't know this name. Do you?'

'I don't know it either, but I haven't read the book.'

Thea knew this, but she felt less anxious when she was able to keep up a stream of chatter. The conversation with Koev in the bathroom was still in her head. As she compared the names, she tried to find a reasonable explanation for what the lieutenant had told her, but she couldn't find one for herself.

'There is no Peev. I crossed it out. Next is Marinov.'

'Okay,' Bobby called. Thea looked at him and saw the weariness in his eyes. He needed to talk too, she thought. She read back through the names she had circled in the book and to her surprise, found not one but two matches.

'There are two people with this last name. I'll colour them red, and then we'll try to figure out who's who.'

'Okay,' Bobby agreed again. This time Thea looked at him like she was waiting for him to explain something to her. 'What? Why are you looking at me like that?'

'Because you just agreed. The Bobby I know does not agree, he analyses.'

'That's right.'

'Bobby?'

'What?'

'You agreed again. What's happening?'

'Hmm.'

'Okay. You obviously need to tell me something, but you don't want to hurt my feelings, or you're very tired, so you are agreeing with everything I say.'

'The first,' Bobby admitted and turned to her.

'Say what you have to say,' insisted Thea.

'Koev is right.'

'What about?'

'Your case is very different from the cases of the other trafficked children.'

'I know that.'

'No, you don't understand. All other children were born in a maternity ward, or there is proof of birth.'

'I have too. Right? All the tests they did proved that I had given birth.'

'But they don't give proof that you gave birth to this exact child,' Bobby tried to explain.

'They will do a DNA test and with that, I will prove that I am the mother.'

'The DNA test will prove that you are close relatives.'

'Bobby, what are you trying to tell me?'

'I already told you, Koev did too, but you don't want to understand it. You will have to go through court to prove that Maria is your daughter. Before the court recognizes that you are the mother, Maria will be just a child without parents.'

Thea looked at him in astonishment, and only then did she realize what the two men had been trying to tell her. Maria wasn't her daughter until proven otherwise, and that wasn't going to happen quickly. Any action she took would be used by the court, her parental rights would be denied, and the child would be given to an adoptive parent.

'There's more,' said Bobby as they stopped at a gas station.

'More?'

'Yes. Even if you prove that you are the mother, the chance that you will be allowed to raise Maria alone is minimal.'

'Why?' Thea asked, but she already knew the answer.

'Because you are without a job, without a home, and your whole family is in custody. And the father of your child ...'

'You don't need to tell me more. I understand.' Thea slouched in the seat and stared ahead. 'How long have you known about this?'

'A week. I have been researching and looking at cases like yours.'

'Let me guess, my guess – my case is exception.'

'It's really rare. I only found one, and unfortunately the mother has been denied all rights over the child. She fought for years, but to no avail.'

'How do you know all this?' Thea asked.

'I talked to her.'

'Have you talked to her face-to-face?'

'Yes. She is sixty-five years old now.'

'Then what happened to her happened last century.'

'Yes. But Thea, I don't think things have changed much since then.'

'And the DNA tests?'

'I told you, Thea, don't get your hopes up. The DNA test will only prove that you are related.'

'Listen, Bobby. You obviously don't know me well. Nothing, absolutely nothing will stop me from fighting for Maria. I will find a way, I will research, I will hire a lawyer ...'

'You're not listening to me, Thea. The moment the judge denies you parental rights, you don't get a second chance. Maria will be adopted, and the secrecy of the adoption will prevent you from contacting her until she comes of age.'

Thea was silent. For the past few months, she had thought that once she found her daughter, everything would be fine. She would find a job and a place to live and raise her. Now Bobby's words seemed to shatter the sky above her, and the clouds broke into small clouds, and those into even smaller clouds, engulfing everything around her. The whole world was black. Her brain refused to comprehend the truth, and her heart seemed to stop. The sound of a heavy book falling to the ground brought her back to reality. In tune with her mood, it was raining outside. Thea stared at the drops running down the car's windshield, then pushed the list Mary had given her off her lap, opened the door, and stepped outside into the rain. Thea saw Bobby get out too, but she motioned for him to get back in the car. She wanted to be alone. The rain was cold and quickly drenched her clothes. Her hair was soaked, and drops of rainwater began to fall from the ends, but Thea paid no attention to them. She was pacing in an imaginary circle, trying to collect her thoughts. How did it come to this?

Koev had called to say that Maria was alive and well and that she was with him now. At that very moment, Thea should have been the happiest mother in the world. And she was internally beaming at this news, but what Koev and Bobby had been trying to explain to her was that finding Maria was irrelevant. Soon someone else would take her, and Thea might never be able to see her. Even now she couldn't pick her up and hug her and kiss her like her daughter. She didn't have the right to do it.

Thea continued to pace, the rain still falling, her thoughts still running. What to do? Who to turn to?

Bobby had honked again. Thea looked at the car and headed that way. She opened the door but did not get inside the car.

'What are the odds? What percentage?' she asked.

'What?' Bobby looked confused.

'You said you had researched these cases. What are the odds? Can you put a percentage figure on it?'

'I don't know. You're better than me at math.'

'Approximately.'

'Very small. I think between 5 and 7 percent.'

Thea shook the water from her hair and sat in the car. 'Drive. I want to see her, at least for a little while.'

Bobby made her put on her seat belt and drove off. The two travelled for a while in silence.

'Why only 5 to 7 percent?' she said, breaking the silence.

Bobby looked at her worriedly before answering. 'Look at the observable facts to a court. The father is a criminal; he sells the child. The child's grandmother, grandfather, and uncle are present at the sale. The mother has no work experience, no qualifications, no job, and no income. She does not have her own home and health insurance. The birth certificate is missing. The mother has no relatives to help her raise the child. I could list more, but I think this gives you a clear idea of why your chance is slim.'

'And if I find a job and rent an apartment?'

'The percentage increases. But I don't know if you will succeed in such a short time.'

'What if I find people to support me? Hypothetically, would this increase my chances?'

'Maybe, but it won't be a deciding factor.'

'What is the deciding factor?'

'You and your past. I think you need to talk to someone in this field, Thea. But you have to prepare yourself mentally for the fact that you might lose your parental rights over Maria sooner than you expected.'

Thea was silent for a while, lost in thought. While they were talking with Bobby a name from earlier came back to her.

'Marinov,' she said quietly. 'It is Marinov, of course.'

'What?' Bobby asked, confused.

'We must call Koev and tell him that it is Marinov.'

'Okay. And who is Marinov?'

'One of Koev's colleagues. That's why they haven't progressed on the cases for so many years. He has covered everything up.'

Thea dialled Koev's phone number and let it ring until he picked up.

'I suspected it was him,' said the lieutenant when he heard the name. He didn't seem surprised.

'How is Maria?' Thea asked.

'Maria is with me. I asked them to take her last so you could see her.'

'Thank you,' she whispered, tears welling up in her eyes again.

Bobby looked at her, then reached out and patted her knee reassuringly. A few minutes later, the two arrived at the place Koev had told them to go to. It was a two-story house, with two cars parked outside. Thea went out and rang the bell. Her hand was shaking with excitement. Footsteps and baby laughter could be heard from inside the house. When the door opened, and Thea saw Maria her worry seemed to disappear. Koev handed her the baby and invited her into the house, directing her to one of the empty rooms.

'I'll leave you alone with her for a few minutes. Please promise me you won't run.'

'I promise,' she said and looked into her daughter's face. Maria was smiling and looking into her eyes. Then she started saying something in her baby language. Thea had dreamed of this moment, and now she just couldn't be happier to be with her. She looked at her, sang to her, talked to her, and Maria smiled at her. Her fingers gripped her hand and sometimes pulled her hair. Thea took a few photos as a keepsake; then she would ask Koev if she could keep them. When he appeared at the door, she turned and hugged Maria as if to protect her.

'She is beautiful, isn't she?' Thea asked.

'Yes,' said Koev. 'She is beautiful.'

Thea kissed her daughter on the head, then with a heavy heart gave her to Koev.

'I will do my best to get her back,' she said and followed him with her eyes as he walked away down the corridor. Koev handed Maria to someone in the room, then returned to Thea and said to her, 'I am convinced of that. I even know who might be able to help us.'

14

The journey back to Sofia was excruciating. Thea was silent, and Bobby, tired from the last few days, concentrated on driving. The rain had picked up again. The streets were flooded, and visibility reduced.

Thea was lost in the memory of meeting her daughter. At first, she felt liberated and calm. Then the worry that she might never see her again came back. According to Bobby, Thea had less than two months to turn things around in her favour, and she had already started thinking about how she could do that. She urgently needed a job and a place to stay. She also needed people to testify in her favour.

'How many people will I have to find to testify in my favour?' Thea said, breaking the silence.

'I don't think the number is important. Rather, you need people who are recognized in society. Doctors, teachers, police officers, people with their own businesses or working in the municipality. People of good social or political standing.'

'You're talking like a journalist right now.'

'I am a journalist.' He smiled.

'I don't know anyone from the above who could appear in court and testify in my favour.'

'Maybe you should talk to Mrs. Mariola,' suggested Bobby.

'She won't agree. I guess she hates me.'

'You have always been her favourite. Maybe if you tell her exactly what happened, she will forgive you.'

'I don't want to bring her into this, Bobby.'

'I don't think you have a choice. Every single person on your side will be useful.'

Thea knew he was right, but the truth was that she was ashamed of her actions and didn't have the courage to stand up to her teacher and ask her for help again.

'Think about it, Thea. In my opinion, you have nothing to lose.'

'I'll think about it,' she said and looked at the rain again. 'Thanks for everything you have done for me, Bobby.'

'Don't thank me. In the end, I will be the beneficiary. I will get one of the most interesting stories in the country.'

'I know you're a good soul and you're not doing it just for your career.'

'That's right. But still, don't forget what you promised me. The story is mine.'

'I won't forget.' She smiled at him and once again drifted into plans about how to increase her chance for parental rights over Maria.

Koev had suggested that Thea stay with Mary for at least a week to make sure her depression wouldn't return. Thea knew that she would not allow herself to do this. There was no time for another bout of depression. She had to focus on finding a job and a place to live. One of Bobby's roommates had given her his old laptop, and Thea had gone deep online in search of information on which jobs worked best for single parents.

'Why don't you try some of the call centres?' Mary had suggested. 'A close friend of mine works from home at a time convenient for her. She is a single mother and only takes chats in the evening. The pay is good.'

Thea took Mary's advice and two days later already had several interviews scheduled. Luckily for her, two of the places were looking for people urgently and wanted to hire her right away, and she agreed. For one call centre she would work during the day and for the other in the evening. Thea couldn't be happier. One week later, she had secured two well-paying contracts.

Finding accommodation was more difficult, as all the landlords were looking for referrals. In the end it was Mary who helped her again. An acquaintance of hers was looking for a roommate, and Thea had proved to be the right fit. Bobby and Koev lent her money and helped her settle into the new apartment.

The moment she secured the accommodation and work contracts, Thea filed an official request for parental rights over Maria. She was devastated to find that Maria had been entered into the system with the name Iliana, a name that Thea never got used to. Bobby had put her in touch with someone who could file all the paperwork and evidence for Thea. Koev had also promised to help her by testifying in her favour. He mentioned that he had found another way to help her, but they would use it only as a last resort. All this would not be enough, however, and Thea knew it. She needed more witnesses, money in the bank, and good references.

'Even if you and Koev stand up for me, it still won't be enough. I need more people who have known me since I was a child and can vouch for me,' she shared with Mary.

'Ask your teacher – she might agree. Go to Bolengrad and talk to the people there.'

'I don't want to go back there, Mary.'

'You have no choice, Thea. You need to find someone to vouch for you. When do you have to provide the evidence in court?'

'I have two more weeks. Maria is currently with a foster family. We managed to stop the process of giving her up for adoption, but my time is short.'

'Swallow your pride and go to Bolengrad. Bobby offered to accompany you.'

'He would do anything to get the story.'

'That's not true and you know it. Bobby is helping you because he's your friend,' said Mary. 'You don't have faith in people, do you?'

'That's right.'

'I know what you went through, and I understand your concerns, but you have to admit that Bobby has nothing to do with Georgi. He will not betray you or your child. Quite the opposite, Thea. Maybe you haven't noticed, but he is the person who helps you the most. To think of him as someone who will betray and use you is not only wrong, but also unfair to him.'

Thea didn't know what to say. Of course, Mary was right, and Bobby had nothing to do with Georgi. But the fear of being used and betrayed again had lodged deep within her, like a storm that was hard to quell. It would take time for her to regain her faith in people.

Still, pressured again by circumstances, Thea accepted Bobby's hand extended to help, and one dark autumn day, the two stopped in front of Mrs. Mariola's house. The teacher knew the purpose of their visit and had agreed to meet Thea only on the condition that there was a witness to the meeting. When she stood on the threshold of the house, Thea felt that comfort and smelled its familiar aroma that she had known for years. This time, however, when the door opened, Mrs. Mariola was not the smiling woman who always greeted her. On the contrary, her arms were crossed in front, and her posture was generally defensive.

'We can talk somewhere else if you want,' suggested Thea.

Mrs. Mariola did not respond to her offer, but only stepped back and gestured for them to enter. Thea, for the first time in her life, felt uncomfortable in this house, and as she walked, she became worried. Her teacher waited for her to sit on the old sofa, then pointed out an empty chair for Bobby, but she herself remained straight. Just like in school, Thea thought. She felt like a schoolgirl about to be tested. The subject of the exam would be her own life.

'First, I would like to apologize for my visit. If it wasn't vitally important to me and my daughter, I wouldn't bother you.'

'So, you didn't think of coming to see me. Asking me what I'm doing or how I am?'

'After our last meeting, I got the impression that I was no longer wanted here,' Thea tried to explain.

'That doesn't stop you from asking someone you say you care about how they're doing, right?'

'No, I guess it doesn't hurt.'

'Okay. So, we've cleared that up. Now I would like to know why this conversation is necessary.'

Thea and Bobby spent an hour trying to explain to Mrs. Mariola how important her testimony would be in court. No matter how hard they tried, the teacher refused to do it.

'I can't help you, Thea. You know I can't lie. My appearance in court will do you more harm than good.'

'Do you hate me that much?' Thea had asked tearfully.

'I don't hate you, but I don't trust you. I wish I could change that feeling, but unfortunately, I can't. I'm sorry, but I can't help you.'

After the meeting, Thea could not sleep and almost stopped eating. She recognised the signs of oncoming depression, and this time she tried her best not to fall into that state.

She was only days away from her court appearance. Though she had never seen the person helping her with her paperwork, they talked often on the phone and via email. He sounded more optimistic with each passing day. However, his positivity never managed to infect Thea.

Missing her daughter, family, and friends made her feel lonely. Thea had grown up in a large family, and the people of the hamlet were always around. Now being alone most of the time in the small flat, without the opportunity to see and talk to people she knew on a daily basis made her feel lonely. She increasingly felt the urge to go and talk to her mother and brother, but everyone told her that until she got custody of Maria, it was the wrong move. She could, however, write to them, and she did.

Lying in bed at night, Thea often wondered how she had gone from a sunny person with prospects to a depressed, gloomy loner. Was fate to blame or her own decisions and actions? Or was it the actions of the people around her? Whatever had caused it, Thea didn't like her new self. She wanted to bring back the sunny and cheerful side of her character and see the sparkle in her eyes again. The fact that she could lose her parental rights over Maria scared her. It made her think that she would have to remain a loner for the rest of her life. What mother could survive such a separation? To know that she was a mum and be unable to prove it was torture. To want to take care of her child, to love her with all her heart, and yet, for some judge to tell her that she was not worthy of it would be a torment.

These dark thoughts were driving her crazy, and although she tried to think optimistically and stand firmly on her feet, Thea knew that the ghosts of her past would decide her fate and the fate of her daughter. And with each passing day bringing her close to her appearance in the courtroom, Thea prayed and cried. Every night she played out what might happen in the courtroom, how she could turn things around and prove that she would be a great mother to her daughter. Every time, however, that black cloud appeared, which split into a hundred pieces and then into a hundred more, and everything around turned black until everything sank into a dark thick fog.

Two days before her court appearance, Thea realized she had given up inside. She was sitting at the kitchen table with an empty glass in her hand and staring blankly ahead. The thought that she had surrendered and the entry of Koev, Mary, and Bobby into the room seemed to happen at the same time.

'Your roommate gave us a key to get in,' Mary said and took the empty glass from her hands.

Thea said nothing. She didn't ask them if they wanted anything to drink or thank them for coming to see her. She had surrendered and her will to live had left her.

Koev approached her and played a recording on her phone. On the video, Thea was standing next to the old well and Georgi was searching her.

'You've done so much, been through so much, and now you're giving up. I want to know why,' Koev asked her. 'Who or what broke you, Thea?'

She looked at him for a moment, then continued to watch the recording.

'You have a real chance to win, Thea,' Mary told her. 'But you have to fight and fight like you did in the beginning. Without fear of losing, without fear of anything.'

Thea continued to watch what was happening by the old well. But Mary's words touched her. She thought about what she had been through to get here.

'There's no way I'm going to win,' she said when the recording ended.

'You have a real chance,' said Bobby. 'You have to stand up and go to court with confidence. To fight for Maria, as you have fought so far. If you lose, I've made a plan for afterwards. Here look at this.'

Bobby handed her a folder. Thea opened the folder, and the first thing she saw was a campaign plan in her support. There were planned dates for posts and events. Two appeals followed, based on new witnesses and evidence if any were found.

'The court told me that I have no right of appeal and that the judge's decision will be final.'

'That's right, but nothing can prevent us from trying to attract a media reaction and to attract people's attention to your case. The fact that your case is unique opens doors that were previously closed,' Bobby tried to explain. 'No one else before you have been in such a situation. The court has no experience with cases like yours, and I think we should take advantage of that.'

Thea's eyes regained their characteristic intelligent gleam. She had started to think positively again.

'The last time you saw your daughter, you promised me that you would fight to the end, Thea.'

'That's right, Koev,' she admitted.

'You still have time to prepare. Nothing is lost yet.'

She got up and poured herself a glass of water. Then she sat back down at the table and looked through the folder Bobby had given her.

'It's not because of the story, is it Bobby?'

'It was never because of journalism. I just don't think it's fair for someone to take your child away.'

Shortly after that, the three of them left, leaving Thea to think about the various options they had offered her in case she lost parental rights.

'Do you remember that I told you that I would help you?' Koev had said to her at the door.

'Yes.'

'What time does your call centre shift end tomorrow?'

'At four o'clock. Why?'

'I will come to pick you up at half past four,' he said and left.

Thea couldn't sleep all night, this time making plans and wondering what Koev was up to. She now remembered that she hadn't asked him what happened to Marinov. Thea had closed herself in her own problems and had not looked outside. She hadn't noticed that her roommate was worried about her. She had missed so much. It was time to get her life back and stop feeling sorry for herself.

When Thea awoke in the morning, the first thing she did was to clean her room and the whole apartment. She washed almost all the clothes she had, sorted the shelves, and watered the flowers. The clean, fresh smells invigorated her. When Thea went into the bathroom, she saw again that sparkle in her eyes that she had lost for a while. Hope had returned. Her life had returned.

Shortly after four o'clock, Koev came to pick her up, and Thea saw satisfaction in his eyes.

'Where are we going?' she asked.

'To prison,' he said.

Thea stopped. 'Why are we going to the prison?'

'I'll tell you on our way,' he replied and quickly walked down the stairs.

As they settled into the car, Thea looked at him questioningly.

'We are going to talk to Georgi,' he said.

'No, no, and no!'

'If you want full custody of Maria, you'll have to talk to him and get him to sign an agreement.'

'Koev, you promised to help me,' Thea said angrily.

'And I will. Let me explain.'

'Okay, I'm listening.'

'I didn't want to tell you about it because I knew you would be worried, so I left it as a last resort. Georgi can be a key witness.'

Thea was surprised. 'But he is in custody.'

'His DNA and yours were found mingled in baby Maria's DNA. He has the same rights as you. We need to get him to give up his parental rights so we can prove you're the mother.'

'We need to hoodwink him?'

'Him and the judge,' laughed Koev.

'You have started to smile more often,' she said.

'We found almost one hundred kids – I have reason to smile. If we can get Maria back to you, I'll smile even more.'

'Okay, what's your plan?'

'We will make an agreement with him. We'll lie to him that if he signs his relinquishment of parental rights, you and Maria will never look for him.'

'And what will happen if he wants me to visit him in prison? You remember the last time you sent me away.'

'He won't want you to visit him.'

'How do you know?'

'I just know.'

'What are you not telling me, Koev?'

'I visited him a week ago and told him that you are planning to marry someone else and that the two of you will raise Maria. He didn't like the news. He said you were a traitor like everyone else, and he didn't want to see you again.'

'What? And who will I get married to?'

'Me.'

Thea was so shocked that her mouth dropped open. She tried to ask a question but didn't know how to phrase it.

Koev smiled. He was obviously enjoying himself. Thea didn't know that side of his character.

'Why should I marry *you*? Why not Bobby, for example? And why do I even have to pretend I'm getting married?'

'Bobby is too comfortable, and I wasn't going to get that reaction out of him. Nor from you.' He laughed again. 'He hates me as much as he hates you. Plus, he and I are the same age, and the idea that you might like someone his age definitely didn't appeal to him.'

'Are you peers? I thought Georgi was younger than you.'

'What does love not do!' Koev laughed again. 'Georgi is one month older than me, but that is actually irrelevant.'

'I really thought he was younger,' said Thea, feeling the surprise must be visible on her face. 'Sorry, I don't mean that you are old. I just can't believe you both are the same age.'

'No problem. Anyway, we're going to meet Georgi with the idea of the two of us being Maria's future parents. We need to get him to sign a document saying that he is giving her up and that you, as her mother, will have no claim on him.'

'What if something goes wrong?'

'If something goes wrong, we will pray that the judge decides in your favour. If it doesn't go in your favour, we'll use Bobby's new media support plan. If that doesn't happen, we'll look for another plan.'

It didn't escape Thea that he used the word *we*. She suddenly wondered if Koev was infatuated with her. The very thought made her dizzy, so she pushed it aside. However, the smiling Koev charmed her, and she continued to look at him, enraptured, until the end of the journey. *What surprises life brings us,* she thought.

15

Their good mood changed when they entered the prison. According to the official documents, Georgi was still under arrest, but after his rampage at the police station, he was moved to prison until his case was over. Thea shuddered at the sounds in the building. This was definitely not a place where she wanted to spend her life.

After Koev signed all the necessary documents to enter, the two were escorted to a room that held several iron tables with benches. Shortly after they sat down at one, the guards brought Georgi to them. His time in prison had changed him. His well-groomed appearance had been replaced with a sloppy one. His beard had grown, and his hair was dishevelled; unusual for him.

Georgi sat opposite them and looked at Thea. His eyes showed hatred and her skin prickled at the sight of them.

'You remember what we talked about last week, right?' Koev said.

'Where do you want me to sign?' said Georgi, continuing to observe Thea.

Koev took out a piece of paper, made Georgi read aloud what was written, and handed him a pen to sign. Thea could feel the tension between the two men. Only now did she realize that Georgi was only looking at her, as if he didn't want to look at Koev. The two men's hatred for each other was so palpable that a guard approached and asked if everything was all right. Georgi signed the document and threw it at Thea.

'One less bastard in this world,' he said and tried to put the pen in his pocket. However, Koev and the guards stopped him.

'Someday I will come back for you, Thea. You can take the child – I don't want it. But you, you, I will want forever and will find you from the other world. If I have to, I will go to hell and come back to get you.'

What he said so surprised Thea and Koev that at first, neither of them reacted. Thea was in the middle of rising from the bench, but Georgi's words had such an impact on her that her legs gave out and she forced herself to sit down again. Koev stared at Georgi as he walked away, and the hand that clutched the pen was shaking violently. They both needed some time to recover from what happened. Finally, Thea collected the signed document and dragged the still-furious Koev outside.

'Are you okay?' he asked her as they drove back from the prison.

'I honestly don't know,' Thea admitted.

'The important thing is that we got him to sign.'

'Yes. But what the hell was that?'

'To be honest, I didn't expect it. I've dealt with a lot of criminals over the years, and over time I've learned to figure them out, but Georgi, he's different. There is something about him, something unpredictable and uncontrollable.'

'I'm afraid of him, Koev.'

'I know. And he knows it.'

'I thought that if I was afraid of him, he would lose interest in me. But now I'm not convinced of that anymore. This man will haunt me as long as I live.'

'Or while he is alive,' Koev said through his teeth. His hatred for Georgi was so obvious that Thea shuddered. In just one day, she was able to see his smiling and hating nature. Until yesterday, she could swear that she did not know a more level-headed person than him. She didn't know what to think or feel now.

16

Two days later, dressed in a nice, business meeting–type dress, Thea headed to the court. At exactly 11 a.m., the judge was going to review all the documents and evidence for her claim for full custody of Maria, or "Iliana" as Sonya had registered her. Thea was prepared to answer questions as well. Mary, Bobby, and Koev were waiting for her in front of the hall. Her roommate Nelly had also come for support. Thea was standing in front of the door of the hall, waiting to be called and she was trembling with tension. Koev stood next to her and held her elbow supportively.

'Stop shaking and calm down if you can. Think of something pleasant.'

'Like what?' she asked, as nothing came to mind.

'When I'm stressed, I think about hot chocolate and biscuits.'

'You're lying,' she said, but she could already smell the hot drink and the cookies.

'I lied, but it has an effect.'

"It does,' she admitted.

At that moment, the door opened, and her name was called. Thea walked in and miraculously felt light and calm. The courtroom was quiet, and she could hear her footsteps. The old wooden parquet floor creaked as she walked on it. Thea thought that the smell inside was the same as the police station in Sofia. It smelled of old wood and sweat.

When the female judge approached, she asked Thea to sit down. Then she took a folder and read from papers contained in it. Behind her, Thea heard the footsteps of the people who had accompanied her into the courtroom. She also heard someone cough in the corridor. Every sound, every page the judge flipped through, unnerved her, and made her jump slightly. The magic of hot chocolate and biscuits had quickly disappeared, and in its place, nervousness had settled in. A few minutes passed, the judge reading something and occasionally glancing over her glasses at Thea. Worried by these looks, Thea turned and looked at Koev. He nodded at her each time and gave her a small smile. As always, he exuded calmness. However, Mary and Bobby were nervous. Both had pursed lips, and their hands were trembling nervously.

'Miss Ivanova, would you please stand up.' The judge's voice startled her.

Thea got up and prepared herself to answer questions.

'I will give your case more time and attention, since it is unusual. I will need a few more documents to help me decide.'

Thea didn't know what to say or do. The judge got up, took the files with her, and left the courtroom. Stunned, Thea stood for a while. Then Bobby approached her and gestured that they should leave the courtroom.

'What happened?' Thea asked.

'The judge needs more documents,' said Koev. 'This is not uncommon in more complex cases.'

'Is this a good or bad sign?'

'I think it's a good sign. She didn't deny you parental rights, so maybe she's considering giving them to you.'

'But when will we know what her decision is?' Thea asked.

'When it comes to a child, it usually takes less time. A month at most,' Mary tried to reassure her.

'One month? I will die of worry until then. And how will I know what documents the judge will need?'

'She didn't mention that you should provide them to her. I think she will most likely demand them from us or the police in Bolengrad. Don't worry, everything will be fine.'

Thea tried to remain upbeat, but her hands began to shake with worry. Somehow, all this waiting and this unknown was causing her agony. Supported by everyone around her, Thea walked out of the building and wondered what she was going to do for a month. Maybe it was a good idea to take extra work hours.

'Don't worry, everything will be fine,' Mary interrupted her thoughts. 'The good news is that if we find someone else to testify in your favour or new evidence, we will be able to add it. In fact, we gained more time.'

'In my opinion, today went well,' added Bobby.

'Thanks for the reassurance. I have to do something during this time. If I have a lot of free time and stay at home, I'll go crazy.'

'Find a hobby,' suggested Koev.

'What kind of hobby?'

'I do not know. Read books, listen to music, sew tapestries, or play sports. Find something to fill your time.'

'I tried to read, but I can't. Music reminds me of the past, and tapestries and sports are not for me.'

'I don't know what else to offer, Thea,' he said, and this time he looked at her with concern. Mary and Bobby had walked ahead to their cars and waved to them before they left.

'Those two get along well,' Koev said and smiled.

'That's right. I keep forgetting how young Bobby really is.'

'He's twenty-two, isn't he?'

'Yes. Can you believe it? I think the last few months have made him grow up. The stories he writes are mostly heavy. But now that I think about it, he was doing that in the provincial newspaper too.'

'You both look and think more maturely than your peers. I keep forgetting how young you really are, Thea.'

'I don't feel young myself.'

The two reached Koev's car. He helped her into the front seat.

'What are your plans for today?' he asked.

'I have none. I was prepared to be happy or upset. But now I don't know what to do.'

'Let me take you to dinner. I want to talk to you about something, but I would prefer to talk somewhere else, not here.'

'Okay,' she agreed and looked at him with puzzlement.

'I'll take you to your apartment to rest, and I'll come pick you up at six.'

'Okay. Where will we go?'

'Somewhere where the cuisine is good and it's cosy.'

Thea thought maybe she should say no, but then she told herself it would be nice to have an evening out. When she got home, she took a shower and, trying to follow Koev's advice, took a book from the shelf in the living room and sat down on the sofa. The book was an interesting crime-love story. A little sweet for her taste, but the story managed to pull her out of reality, and when she looked at the clock at one point, she saw that she was getting late and Koev would be coming soon. Luckily for her, he was also late. Twenty minutes after six, Koev appeared at the door, this time wearing jeans and a sports sweater. Thea had mostly seen him dressed in a shirt and suit, and his casual appearance surprised her.

'Are we going to watch a match?' she asked.

'No. I told you – we're having dinner.'

Thea took her handbag and walked out with him into the cold corridor of the block. As they walked down the stairs, he told her that the judge had requested documents from the Bolengrad Police, mostly witness statements for the day after the birth.

'What witness statements?'

'I think those of the medical team that did the tests.'

'This is a good sign, isn't it?'

'I think so,' Koev said and helped her get into the car again. 'The restaurant we will go to is outside Sofia. I hope you don't mind if we make a longer trip.'

'On the contrary, I think it will have a refreshing effect on me.'

Thea stared at the buildings as they passed. The weather was warm for the season, and many people were out for a walk. It was that time of day when night prevailed. By the time they got out of the city, it was almost dark. Thea was not bothered by the darkness; she felt safe in Koev's presence. He was like her guardian angel. Always nearby and always helpful.

'What are you thinking about?' he asked.

'I was thinking about you,' she admitted.

Koev smiled again.

'And what do you think about me?'

'That you are always nearby and always find a way to help me. Even now.'

'And what exactly am I doing now?'

'You are taking me far away so that I don't cling to my gloomy thoughts.'

'Is that what you would have done if you had spent the evening alone?' he asked, briefly glancing at her.

'Most likely, yes. I followed your advice and read a book this afternoon.'

'Did you like the book?'

'Somewhat. I liked the crime part, but the love story was kind of over the top. No one loves someone so much that they would change their life for them.'

'Hmm.'

'What? Don't you agree?'

'I don't agree.'

'Have you changed your life for someone you love?'

'Actually not.'

'Then why don't you agree?'

'Because I know a lot of people who did it, including you. Didn't you change your life because of Georgi?'

Thea said nothing. Of course, Koev was right again. She had been young and very, very much in love. She would have done anything Georgi wanted.

'How did the book end?' asked Koev.

'I don't know, I haven't got there yet, but I have a feeling it will be one of those stories with a happy ending.'

'Great. That's what you need. Anyway, we've arrived.'

Thea looked out and saw that they had stopped in front of a tavern.

'Here they make one of the tastiest chicken soups I've ever eaten. In general, their cuisine is very good.'

Thea got out of the car, waited for Koev to approach her, and they both entered the warm pub. He headed straight for a table in the corner and gestured for the waiter to come over. There were not many people in the tavern, but Koev explained to her that Tuesdays were like that, not busy. The music was soft, and Thea liked that. After they ordered, she looked at the smiling Koev. He had changed in the last few weeks.

'You're looking at me like that again,' he told her.

'How?'

'Exploratory. Is there something wrong?'

'I don't know. You look different to me. Calmer and in a good mood. You also took me out for dinner.'

'It's not a romantic dinner, in case you're wondering. I just think you deserve a little entertainment, a little variety if you want to call it that.'

'Why do you help me so much, Koev?' she asked, looking into his eyes. Eyes never lie.

Koev didn't answer right away. He didn't look away, and she saw concern and warmth in his eyes. Some deep feeling that she couldn't explain because no one had ever looked at her like that before.

'It is difficult for me to answer your question,' he said at last. Then he leaned back and looked at her again. 'But I'll try,' he added thoughtfully.

The waiter came and left drinks and salad on their table. This interrupted their conversation somewhat.

'I know everyone tells you this, but for me your story is extraordinary. Your desire to find Maria and dedication to doing everything possible to get her back impressed me. Honestly, I don't know another person like you. That's why I'm helping you, and that's why I want everything to end well for you. Let me admit something to you. At first, I thought you were lying.'

Thea was amazed. 'You didn't believe me?'

'Not at all. When I suggested you come back to the hamlet, I didn't expect you to accept. Your decision surprised me so much that it caught me off guard.'

Koev smiled at the memory. 'When I saw you for the first time at the police station, I thought you would act like everyone else. I thought you would get scared and withdraw your complaint. However, in time, I realized how wrong my first impression of you was. Not that the people who knew you didn't warn me. Everyone claimed that you were different from the people in the hamlet, that you were smart and moral. I didn't believe them until I got to know you better. You have earned my trust and respect. And that is not easy for a person like me. That's why I'm helping you.'

Thea nodded, then started to ask something else, but the waiter cut her off again. When he walked away, she seemed to forget the question she wanted to ask.

'I love this soup,' said Koev, smiling. He tore off a piece of the bread and began to eat. Thea also focused on her food.

'You wanted to ask me something else.'

'Yes. You said you wanted to talk to me about something.'

'Actually, I don't think it's a good idea to talk about it now. Let's enjoy the food and the setting.'

'Okay, you can tell me on the way to Sofia... I was thinking about Sonya.'

'What about her?'

'Did she say why she took those four children with her?'

'Actually, her explanation was very good. Georgi gave them the addresses of the "new parents", but before they gave the babies to them, Sonya's husband researched them. According to her, the children would have fallen into very bad hands. During the interview, she gave us the names and addresses, and Mary and I were able to research them. I wouldn't entrust a child to these people, especially the ones Maria was supposed to go to.'

'Why? Are they criminals?'

'Thea, some criminals are wonderful mothers and fathers. I have seen their children cry for them when they are arrested. No, the ones these kids should have gone to were psychopaths. It may seem incredible to you, but I believe that Sonya saved their lives.'

'By kidnapping them and leading them away? Do you want to justify her actions?'

'No, she will be tried for child abduction and trafficking, but that doesn't change the fact that she took good care of these children and didn't let anything worse happen to them.'

'Please, don't tell me I have to send her a thank you letter. She was at Tanya's, she could have contacted the police, but she didn't.'

Koev raised his voice. 'You forget who worked in our department until recently.'

This startled Thea and she admitted to herself that he was right. Sonya had been placed in a very delicate position, and in fact she should have been grateful that this woman had taken Maria with her.

'I'm sorry, I didn't want to be rude,' said Koev. 'The idea tonight was to cheer you up.'

'No, you're right. Now that I think about it, Sonya hardly had any other choice. Once you get involved with these people, it's hard to let go. Maybe I'll visit Sonya one day.'

'It would be nice if you did. She wants to talk to you about it herself.'

Thea nodded and turned her attention back to the food.

'It's delicious, isn't it?'

'It is,' she answered, and she really meant it.

'We can come here every Tuesday,' Koev suggested.

'Even after the judge's decision?' Thea was surprised.

'Even after that if you want. Having dinner once a week with a good friend is something I've been dreaming of for years.'

'Aren't you having dinner with your friend the private investigator?'

'Not as often as either of us would like. He is a busy man and spends more time with women and drinking than with his friends.'

'I forgot to thank you for hiring him to help me. I never found out if he discovered anything.'

'In fact, he has made a very detailed study of Georgi and your family. As well as of you. His report is in one of the folders the judge is looking at.'

'May I read the report?' Thea asked, and she immediately noticed Koev's concern.

'I don't know if it's a good idea, Thea,' he said and called the waiter over, as if to avoid the subject.

'Why would that be a bad idea?'

'Because you won't like the things he recorded about your family. Look, I think it's better if you don't think about it now. Better focus on yourself and Maria.'

'Don't you think it's better for me to know?' Thea insisted.

'On the contrary, I think you should read the report someday, but I don't think now is the time. The information in it may'—Koev hesitated— 'shock you.'

'You think I won't be able to take it?'

'If you are asking for my honest opinion, no. I don't think you will be able to bear what is written in the report and it will depress you. That is not what you need this month as you wait for the outcome of the court case.'

Thea watched him. His smile was gone. In front of her again stood her familiar Koev. Concerned but business-like. He was looking her straight in the eye as if begging her not to ask him any more questions.

'Okay,' she agreed. 'I will read the report after the judge's decision.'

Koev breathed a sigh of relief. Then he handed her the dessert menus.

'Can I ask you just one more question?'

'Ask.'

'I sometimes feel like you know exactly how I feel. What have you been through?'

Koev's body stiffened, and his gaze darkened again with tension. He turned the dessert menu around for a while, then set it down on the table and looked at Thea.

'Let's not talk about it now.'

'Okay,' she agreed and smiled at him. Whatever he had been through had hardly been easy, Thea was sure of that. She chose a dessert, waited for him to order it, and turned the conversation to everyday things – her work, the weather, anything to distract them from the tense atmosphere.

When they left the tavern, Thea felt calm and invigorated. She had really liked the food and admitted to herself that she would look forward to next Tuesday with Koev and coming here again. On the way back to Sofia, they hardly spoke. She was tired from the emotional day, and he was focused on driving in the dark.

After she got home, Thea fell asleep almost instantly, and for the first time in months, she didn't have nightmares.

17

Thea's days slipped by imperceptibly. She had taken on extra hours to fill her time. She didn't want to have time to think and wanted to be busy all the time. Every morning, Thea woke up thinking about her daughter, wanting all this waiting to finally end and for the judge to make a decision. However, there was no news from the court, either in the first or second week. Koev called her almost every day to ask how she was doing. On Tuesdays he came to pick her up, and the two of them spent several hours in the cosy tavern, talking both the news surrounding her case and everything else that was happening around them. Thea read a lot of books and often told him about the stories in them, and he sometimes told her about the cases he had worked on.

In the middle of the third week, the judge relayed that she had made a decision and set a date on which she would announce it. When she heard the news, Thea's heart sank. She stopped sleeping and eating again. Books didn't help her anxiety, and Nelly, worried about her again, had called her friends. Mary and Bobby visited her during the day, trying to cheer her up, but it didn't work. Koev also spoke to her on the phone. He had taken a big case and had to leave Sofia. Talking to him also failed to calm her down. The thought that she might be stripped of her parental rights and separated from her daughter forever depressed her. Panic had worked its way into her mind, and Thea had several panic attacks. Nelly eventually took her to the hospital.

'What are you doing to yourself, Thea?' Bobby asked her when he visited her. 'Getting psyched isn't going to help you. Try to think positively.'

'I tried.'

'You have to try harder. Go outside or read love novels. Working for call centres twelve hours a day is not going to help you.'

'How do you know how many hours I work?'

'Nelly told me. She's worried about you. She found you passed out on the floor in the bathroom. How do you think this affects her?

Thea knew Bobby was right. She had to pull herself together, stop drinking coffee 24/7, and cut back on her work hours.

'I promise to try harder,' she said and tried to smile.

●●

The next day she was discharged, and Mary visited her at home with the same recommendations as Bobby.

'In three days, you will know what the judge's decision is, and all this will be over,' she told her.

Thea wondered how to spend those three days without going crazy. Koev rarely called her anymore. He was busy with the new case he had taken on, and from what he had told her, Thea knew it was about something terrible that had happened to several children. His dark mood had returned again, and though he tried to joke at times, she could feel the strain of his work.

Two days before the judge's decision, Koev rang the doorbell, asked her to dress up, and the two of them went to the cosy tavern.

'On Friday it's busy, but I managed to book a table for us,' he said while driving. His smile had returned, and Thea had no doubt that he had solved the case he had been working on.

'Are we going to have dinner there twice a week, or is today an exception?'

'With my job, it's amazing that I manage to come every Tuesday,' he said. 'Not that I would refuse to come here on Fridays with you. This is like an oasis for us, don't you think?'

'Yes. It is nice to escape here.'

'I'm sorry I haven't been around for the past ten days. I only found out you were in the hospital yesterday. Mary doesn't work in my department anymore; she got promoted, I guess you know.'

'No, I didn't know. She failed to tell me.'

'She's very busy. Anyway, I've taken a few days off until next Wednesday, and I think it would be good for you to also rest for a few days before you appear in court.'

'I'm fine,' Thea said as they entered the tavern. They sat down at the table reserved for them and ordered the usual food.

'You don't look good, Thea. That's why I took a few days off. I think it's good for both of us to rest. I'm tired too.'

'And what do you want us to do for the next two days?' she asked.

'We will go skiing on Vitosha.' He smiled.

'What? I cannot ski.'

'To be honest, I can't either, but if other amateurs can do it, it shouldn't be that hard, right?'

'I like the idea of going to climb Vitosha, but not the skiing part.'

'Then we'll just take the lift to the Aleko hut and walk around. How does that sound to you?'

Thea smiled. 'Sounds good.'

'You have to calm down, and you must be confident in court, Thea.'

'I know, but the very thought of going there makes me nervous. I can't stop thinking about it. I can't stop thinking about Maria and wondering where she is now, who is taking care of her.'

'You can't help but worry about her. It's completely understandable. I think all mothers think about their children, and you are no exception.'

'I also think about my family, about the hamlet, about my friends there. What will happen to them?'

'You can't worry about everyone, Thea. Especially now. You better calm down, and I know everyone is telling you, but I'll say it too – think positive. Imagine that the judge decides to give you full custody of Maria. What are you going to do then? Do you have a plan? Where will you live, and how will you take care of her?'

'Oh, I have a plan. I spend whole nights thinking about it. I'll take her to live with me. I've already spoken to Nelly, and she doesn't mind.'

'And the landlord?'

'I will only talk to them if they return Maria to me.'

'And what will happen if the landlord does not agree? Do you have plan B?' Koev asked.

'No,' she admitted.

'This is what I wanted to talk to you about the first time I brought you here. Finding accommodation for a single mother with a baby is very difficult. Some of my colleagues have this problem. For some reason, most landlords don't want children and animals on their properties, which I think is crazy and unfair, but it's the reality.'

'I'll still find somewhere.'

'Maybe, or maybe you won't have to look.'

'What do you mean?' she asked.

'I don't know how you will accept my offer, but you can stay with me. My apartment is big, and as you know, I rarely go home.'

What Koev said surprised her. 'Do you want me to move in with you?'

'Yes.'

'But ...' Thea was shocked by the offer and didn't know how to respond. Koev saw her confusion and tried to say something, but she stopped him, got up and went to the toilet. As she walked, she felt her legs grow weaker, and after two steps, she collapsed to the ground. Then she heard the people around her fussing and running to help her. Someone was leaning over her and asking her questions, but for some reason, she couldn't answer. It was like her mouth was stuck. Then Thea smelled Koev's aftershave, felt him carry her in his arms and to the car. It was a strange feeling to hear and feel everything but be mute and weightless.

Koev took her to the urgent care centre and stayed with her while she was being examined.

'You will be fine,' he told her and squeezed her hand from time to time. Thea tried to squeeze back, but she had no strength. It was as if something had paralyzed her. She could hear, she could see somewhat, but she could not move. At one point she felt tired and fell asleep. When she woke up a few hours later, Thea saw Koev sleeping in the chair next to her. His body had slid down. *The chair isn't comfortable*, Thea thought. Then she tried to get up but cried out from the pain she felt in her lower back. Koev was startled by her cry and fell to the floor. Then he stood up and leaned over her.

'Are you okay?' he asked worriedly.

'Yes.'

Koev nodded and rang the bell to call the nurse.

'The doctor said you probably have a side effect reaction from the panic attacks. With rest and painkillers, you will be fine.'

'And the pain in my lower back?'

'It's from the fall. They did an X-ray; nothing is broken, it's just bruised.'

'Apparently, I won't be skiing tomorrow.'

'Yes, we will postpone it for another day.'

The nurse came into the room and gave her a routine exam. 'You need to rest,' she advised Thea and left the room.

Koev stood by the bed and hesitated about what to do.

'Go home and rest,' Thea told him. 'The chair doesn't look very comfortable.'

'Thea, I'm sorry about … you know.'

'No problem. Let's talk about it tomorrow, shall we?' she suggested.

'Okay. I will come at noon to see you. I will also bring you food because you know what the food is like in hospital.'

Thea nodded wearily and began drifting off again.

18

When Thea woke up in the morning, she saw that it was just about dawn. She could hear footsteps in the corridor, and the woman in the next bed was snoring loudly. It was a typical hospital setting. She tried to stand up, and this time the pain in her lower back was bearable. She managed to move to the chair that Koev had slept on, and looked out the window, watching the slowly waking city. It reminded her of that far-off day when she had watched the street traffic through the window of Mary's office suite. A lot had happened since then, she thought, and, as they did every morning, her thoughts turned to Maria. Does she sleep late in the morning? What do they give her for breakfast? Is there someone to cover her up at night? There were a thousand questions in her head every morning.

Thea stared at the rising sun and wondered what would happen today. What would happen tomorrow, and most importantly, what would happen the day after? What did fate have in store for her? One thing was clear – Thea hadn't expected to wake up in a hospital today. She hadn't expected Koev's proposal either. Why was she so shocked, she wondered. Now that she thought about it, he had offered her his help, he had offered her shelter for her and her daughter, nothing more. Hadn't she over-thought it? And she hadn't found out his true intentions. Thea hadn't asked him, hadn't given him a chance to explain. The truth was, she was afraid to find out. In her heart, Thea knew that Koev was very much in love with her. Phone calls, Tuesdays at the tavern, his looks and touches were proof of that. But it wasn't his feelings that bothered her; it was hers. She only now realized that she had been doing her best to suppress her own attraction to him for a long time. She considered it rash and wrong and tried not to think about it. However, his proposal yesterday shocked her. Not what he said, but what she assumed. Now, watching the sunrise, Thea felt more confused and uncertain than ever. She didn't know what to do, what to say to him.

Thea slowly got up from the chair and went back to bed. She tried not to think about anything and stared at the ceiling, looking for cracks somewhere, like she used to do when she was a child in her father's house. It wasn't long before the hospital staff started going around the rooms, doing the routine check-ups and handing out medicine. Then they called everyone to breakfast, and somehow Thea's morning passed without giving in to her worries and thoughts. Shortly before noon, the doctor told her that if she felt well, she could go home, and Thea gladly accepted the offer. Around lunchtime, while they were preparing her documents, Koev seemed to arrive just in time.

'I brought you lunch, but I see that you are already ready to go home.'

'I will not refuse good food,' she said and tried to smile.

'Okay. Do you want me to drive you to your flat?' he asked uncertainly.

'Yes. We can talk while you drive.'

Koev nodded, helped her gather her things, and helped her walk to the parking lot. Although the pain in her lower back had subsided, Thea still found it difficult to walk.

'Let's talk first,' she said when they got into the car.

'Okay.' Koev turned to her and tried to say something else, but she stopped him.

'Thank you for taking care of me,' she said. 'I know I've told you this before, but I really mean it. And thanks for the suggestion that Maria and I move in with you. I honestly didn't expect it.'

Thea looked away and swallowed hard.

'My life is very confused, Koev. So confused! I don't know who to trust and who not to. I don't know what to expect from tomorrow. Most of the time, I'm so scared to think about the future that it takes my breath away. So, let's leave it at that for now. Let's hear what the judge's decision will be. I am convinced that immediately after this decision, my life will probably be in order.'

'What are you trying to tell me, Thea?'

'That this between us, whatever it is, will have to wait and that I am not ready for this conversation, although I feel that you are.'

Koev looked away. 'You understand,' he said quietly.

'Yes. You too.'

He sighed, then looked at her. 'You're right let's not talk about our feelings now. I think you need good food and rest today and tomorrow. I'll take you to your flat and let you calm down. But if you need anything, you'll call me, right?'

'I will call you – I promise.'

'Good,' said Koev. He put on his seat belt, waited for her to put on hers, and started the car. On the way, they were both silent, each lost in thought. Thea was thinking of a warm shower and a good book. She would spend two days in bed. When they arrived, Koev helped her into the flat, then, despite her protests, went to the nearby supermarket to buy her food. He cared for her like no one else had before, Thea thought.

Thea did not leave the apartment for two days. She decided to work so that she would have no time and opportunity to think. She had spoken to Koev twice, but their conversations had not gone well. Something had snapped between them. It was as if they had both stopped talking at some point. The strange thing was that even though both of them were silent on the phone, they could not bear to hang up.

On the day the judge was to announce her decision, Thea decided to use public transport. When she arrived at the court her friends were waiting for her, and everyone wished her success. Koev told her that she looked rested and gave her an encouraging smile. At that moment, her name was called, and Thea walked unsteadily towards the judge. The woman had put on her glasses and was watching her approach. Thea could feel her searching gaze, and her heart beat faster. When she was close enough, she stopped and waited for the judge's instructions.

'You can stay standing if you want. I am ready with my decision, but before I give it, I want to express my regret for everything that happened to you and your child. It took me several weeks to read every piece of evidence and every document, and I must admit I was very confused. Your family and the father of your child have criminal records, but everyone says you're not a criminal. I wonder, Miss Ivanova, if this is really so or if you are very clever to be able to lie to everyone and get away with it. You are smart – there is no doubt about that. Everyone says so, and your success in school proves it. But are you a good person? I had a harder time finding proof of this.'

The judge fell silent, her gaze on Thea.

'Are you a good person, Miss Ivanova?'

It was hard for Thea to speak; her mouth was dry.

'I don't know. A person's opinion of herself usually differs from the opinion of others about her.'

The judge nodded. 'That's right. I read a lot of recommendations for you. What I'm asking you is, how do you define yourself?'

'I'm trying to be a good person, my lady,' Thea answered.

The judge continued to look at her quizzically, and Thea wished the floor would open up so she could sink into it, out of sight behind the glasses.

'Are you ready to hear my decision, Miss Ivanova?'

'Yes,' said Thea and felt dizzy.

'I give you full parental rights over Iliana Georgieva Stamenova.'

Tears welled in Thea's eyes when she heard this. Her legs seemed to go limp, and her body folded in two. Thea was crying with relief as she crouched in front of the judge's bench. The woman watched her and gave her time to recover.

'Thank you! Thank you so much!' said Thea.

'I'm not done. There are two conditions to my decision. One is that you will be monitored monthly on how you care for the child for the next two years. My other condition is that this child never sets foot in the place where she was born. Do you understand my conditions, Miss Ivanova?'

'Yes, my lady.'

'Within three days, the child will be handed over to your care. Use this time to prepare the home you live in for her stay there.'

'I will, my lady.'

'Good luck, and don't make me regret my decision,' said the judge. She then took the files and left.

Thea had never felt so happy. Koev approached her and hugged her. Mary and Bobby also joined them, excited by what they had heard.

'What a story,' said Bobby, and everyone laughed.

Thea's excitement quickly turned to worry about whether she would be able to prepare everything she needed for her daughter. What worried her the most was the reaction of her landlord. Would they let her, and Maria – Iliana – stay in the flat?

Thea and her friends were leaving the courtroom when a young woman stopped them and handed her a sheet of instructions for everything the child would need. Thea read the things listed, and when she finished, her hand began to shake. One of the requirements was to have a separate room for the child. She hadn't expected this.

'Such are the standards for adoption,' Mary explained.

'But this means that I have to rent an independent apartment.' Thea began to despair. She wouldn't be able to work during the day because she had to take care of Maria. Her salary wouldn't cover the rent, and everything needed for the baby. She would think of something, Thea decided, and smiled happily at the news that Maria would soon be with her.

After sharing a brief treat with her friends, and promising Bobby that she would meet soon to discuss his article, Thea returned to the flat and began making a list of the clothes and supplies she needed to welcome her baby. She left the problem of lodging for last. As soon as she was done with the list, Thea called Koev.

'Do you want to talk?'

'Yes,' he agreed, but she sensed uncertainty in his voice.

Neither of them spoke, and there was an awkward silence on the line. Thea quietly cried, not knowing what to say, so she just hung up the phone. She felt miserable and stupid. She lay down on her bed, hugged the pillow, and sobbed with all her heart. What the hell was going on with her life? She got her daughter, her most precious one, and now they had nowhere to live. Koev's lack of sympathy and understanding made her even more desperate. She had relied on his help for too long. She had become attached to him, and on a day like today, she had imagined that he would be by her side. The happiest day of her life quickly turned into a nightmare. Where would she go, and what would she do? Thea tried to come up with a solution.

Thea heard Nelly coming home and tried to calm down but couldn't. Lying in bed and clutching the pillow, she continued to sob softly. Her roommate knocked on the door of the room, waited for a while, then left. Shortly after, Thea heard footsteps approaching again, but the footsteps were definitely not Nelly's. Someone knocked again. Thea hesitated to open the door but finally did. To her surprise, Koev was standing in front of her with a large bag full of baby things.

'Why are you crying?' he asked her. 'And why didn't you pick up the phone? Did something happen to Maria?'

'Nothing happened to Maria. I just ...' She took his hand and made him sit on the chair. 'I wanted to talk to you. It's not about my daughter; it's about me and you.'

Koev was visibly worried. Her hand was still in his; she tried to pull it away, but he held her back.

'It's not easy, isn't it?' he said quietly. 'We are so much alike. We have been hurt so many times in the past, and it is hard for us to even trust each other. It's hard for us to even talk about it.'

Thea released her hand, took a chair, and sat next to him. 'I'm afraid, Koev.'

'I know.'

'Are you afraid?'

'Feelings are a complicated thing, Thea. Sometimes it takes time to figure out exactly what we're feeling and why.'

'Do you need more time?'

'No, not really. And you?'

'Perhaps.'

'So, you won't accept my offer?' he asked.

'On the contrary.'

'But ...' Koev looked at her questioningly. Thea nodded. He stared at her, first hesitantly as if he didn't understand, then Koev's eyes sparkled, and he smiled that warm smile of his.

'Come, let me show you my apartment,' he offered, taking her hand, and helping her to her feet. Thea followed, and a few days later, when her daughter was handed over to her, she thought she had made the right decision. She finally felt truly happy.

Maria had grown up in the time since she had last seen her. The moment Thea hugged her again, she felt that affection, that inexplicable feeling that had come over her at birth. A mother's love that could not be replaced by anything else in the world. She smiled at her daughter, hugged her even tighter, and thought about the turning points in her life. 'There is no complete happiness,' her grandmother had told her as a child, but looking now at Koev and her daughter, Thea told herself that her grandmother was wrong. There is complete happiness, and she had proof of it. Here and now, in this room and at this moment, she felt it with all her heart and soul.

Also by Hristina Bloomfield

DEEPLY IN THE SOUL

"Deeply in the Soul" (2022) - 5 stars Readers' Favorite,

Honorable Mentions at the 2023 Hollywood Book Festival,

Honorable Mentions at the Paris Book Festival 2023

Xena is forced to run away when she finds out her boyfriend sold her. After years of running, her past finally catches up with her...

The story follows Xena who finds herself in the situation of a victim but manages to escape. After her boyfriend is unable to return a loan, she is sold to the moneylender who wants her to work for him as a prostitute. She flees her hometown and tries to start a new life, but her past keeps catching up with her. Xena struggles to find her way as each time she gets to a good place, she has to run again. After months of solitude, Xena finally trusts Agent Dobrevski who helps Xena to face her trauma in order to finally live a normal life. The story begins in a small mountain town in Eastern Europe and ends in Cornwall, UK.

Deeply in the Soul is crime fiction; however, it also includes themes such as trauma, grief, romance, action and friendship. Xena's story is not only tragic but inspirational too. She is a survivor.

Becky

"Becky" (2022) 5 stars Readers' Favorite.

Her life will pass through your fingers as you read this book.

Sixteen-year-old Becky is raped and left lying with multiple stab wounds on the Cornwall coast. Instead of supporting and helping her in this difficult time, her parents send her to London, where her cousin Arnie promises to take care of her. Arnie and his roommates Paul and Alex help her recover. When the police fail to find the perpetrators, the three men hire private detectives to help with the investigation. Becky accepts their help and in time, she and the lawyer Alex become very good friends. The difficulties they have to go through even bring them closer together. Becky and Alex fight both against her abusers and against her family, which keeps causing her trouble. After many vicissitudes, Becky finally finds justice. But fate does not let her enjoy her new life. She experiences loss after loss.

Becky's story has pain and betrayal as well as friendship, hope, and very strong love, the loss of which will be difficult for her.

Kurt

Books's awards and stickers

"Kurt" (2023) 5 stars Golden sticker from Reader View,

Honorable Mentions at the 2023 Hollywood Book Festival

Honorable Mentions at the Paris Book Festival 2023

His music, his dog Dante, and his motorcycle were his life until one day everything changed.

Fifty-six-year-old rock star Kurt and his rock band set up to create their new album in Cornwall. They are joined by the lyricist Leah, who agrees to help them with the lyrics for the new songs. Everything is going well until one night one of the band's roadie and Leah's taxi driver are killed. Clues led to two different killers. One wants to kill Kurt and the other Leah. Then both are subsequently shot by a sniper.

The investigation was unsuccessful, and the police inspectors send Leah far away and use Kurt to get the killers to show up.

However, new revelations about Leah's identity confuse the musician. Kurt's life will turn in an unexpected direction for him, and new revelations will make Kurt realize that he has unwittingly intervened in something from which he will hardly be able to escape.

Printed in Great Britain
by Amazon

58696032R00128